THE SUFI FIDDLE

THE

Sufi

FIDDLE

Richard Bulliet

St. Martin's Press

New York

Design by Susan Hood

Library of Congress Cataloging-in-Publication Data

Bulliet, Richard W.
     The Sufi fiddle / Richard Bulliet.
        p.   cm.
   ISBN 0-312-04852-1
   I. Title.
  PS3552.U44S8 1991
  813'.54—dc20   90-49313
                               CIP

First Edition: February 1991
10 9 8 7 6 5 4 3 2 1

For Lucianne

THE SUFI FIDDLE

Prologue

A gibbous moon reproduced its image on the circular floor of a stone fortress looming high like a midnight galleon upon a rippling sea of dark date palms. The space sheltered within the fortress's crenellated parapet was mostly moonlit, leaving only a crescent of shadow on the western side. Doorways atop staircases rising from lower levels cast smaller, triangular shadows. Smaller still were the irregular patches of dark next to the two dozen turbaned men kneeling motionless on the stones. Only one shadow moved.

Shaykh Zakariya Pahlavani, grizzled, spade-bearded, said to be eighty years old, stood swaying within the semicircle of his kneeling disciples, bowing his violin. Brighter light would have revealed faces of many types—old and young, clean-shaven and bearded, Asian, African, Caucasian—but all with a common look of inner stillness and concentration. Their shaykh had summoned them, the spiritually gifted, the most elevated adepts from the far-flung chapters of the Pahlavani Sufi brotherhood of which the shaykh was master. He had not explained his summons. His disciples' obedience to their master prevented them from asking. Yet they all knew. The shaykh was preparing to choose his successor.

The disciples had lived together for a week, communing in their five daily prayers, taking simple meals in a large room deep within the fortress, and sleeping in separate stone cells. The shaykh had received each of them privately. Each had knelt before him on a straw mat. Some had met him many times before, some only seldom. To some he spoke gentle words of guidance. Some he plied with searching questions. Some interviews were entirely silent.

This final evening, a Thursday, they had supped on bread and cheese and then washed their hands, feet, and faces. A few had trimmed beards or nails. As on previous nights, they had gathered on the top floor of the fortress in a semicircle around the shaykh, their small group itself encircled by the lofty parapet that hid everything from view but the moon and the stars. Three water pipes, each topped by a glowing coal nested on a mixture of tobacco and hashish, circulated among them, each man inhaling the smoke three times before passing the mouthpiece to his brother.

For half an hour, in rhythmic unison, the disciples chanted "Allah," the name of God. For another half hour they collectively exhaled the single syllable *"hu,"* meaning "He." When Shaykh Zakariya saw in their faces the signs of entrancement in a common mystic vision, he stood and began to play.

None of them could or would have described the music because they experienced it with their souls more than with their ears, and the music of paradise is indescribable. Those least advanced on the mystic path, including a tall bearded black man and a short, wiry, bespectacled man beside him, experienced total paralysis. Whether they were physically able to move was untestable because their wills were in thrall to the music, and movement was beyond conception. A larger number listened and then, one by one, rose to dance. Their dance was a slow turning with arms outstretched and heads reclining toward the right shoulder. Instead of being overpowered by the music, they entered into it—not by adopting its rhythm, for their rates of rotation varied and bore no relation to the sounds, but by moving in empathy with the vision evoked in each man's mind by the ethereal strains.

Two men continued kneeling in humble obedience, neither paralyzed by the music nor succumbing to the urge to dance. Zaid, an Arab of middle age and the shaykh's companion of twenty years, had of late also become his deputy on those increasingly frequent occasions when physical infirmity kept the shaykh from leading the seances. The other, Moosa Makki, was a younger, ferociously mustached American, a convert to Islam who had but recently gained the shaykh's attention because of his amazingly precocious spiritual attainment.

Despite his demeanor of contemplative repose, Moosa Makki's mind was neither contemplative nor quiet. It was still reeling from what the shaykh had told him in private before their meager supper. So it would be Zaid! Sober, loyal Zaid. The favorite, the intimate. A man with only a fraction of Moosa's mind, only a scintilla of Moosa's spiritual vision.

"Moosa," Shaykh Zakariya had said, "Zaid is far less than you, but his heart is pure. To control the music without being controlled by it is the final step. You took it in a giant leap after a short, intense run. Zaid took it in a final tiny movement after a lifetime of inching forward. Your leap has already carried you far beyond Zaid, and Zaid has reached the end of his path. But Zaid is of pure heart, and you are not."

Moosa had remained kneeling, forcing himself to accept the terrible judgment with unclouded composure.

"To control the music is to wield power, Moosa. Not mortal power, but the power of God's spirit. The person with a black spot in his heart cannot keep that power from corrupting him. I know. The black spot in my heart was too small for my master to see, but I have become corrupt. Your black spot is larger." The shaykh paused and studied the obedient figure before him. "Zaid has a pure heart, Moosa," he said gently. "I shall make the next violin for him."

The shaykh's final words echoed and re-echoed in Moosa's mind, yet he willed himself to stillness on the cold stones just as he had found the inner strength to rise above the violin's music and make its power his own. When the seance ended, Moosa made his way alone to his cell. Two hours later he reemerged.

It wasn't hard to steal the violin. Shaykh Zakariya slept soundly on his back, emitting rasping breaths from his gaping black mouth.

Moosa Makki stole away into the night. With him went the tall bearded black man and his small, wiry companion.

1

Grand juryman Winter gazed at the back of the head of the woman seated in front of him. Her temples were shaved smooth to an inch and a half above her ears. Her auburn hair, swept up and back as if windblown, tumbled down in artful turbulence, tapering to a pointed tail descending some six inches down the center of her back. Winter tried to avoid staring continuously, but the rapture of contemplating her exotic cranium had slowly become his only diversion from his bleak surroundings. He tore his imagination away with an effort when he found it wandering too boldly in a lustful direction. Instead he braced his elbows and body against the red leather of the chair and surrendered his eyelids to gravity. The deep, bored voice of an assistant district attorney flowed over him like warm, sulfurous mud.

"I deem this eight-by-eleven-inch piece of paper in evidence as Grand Jury Exhibit Two. Reading from the lower right-hand corner of Grand Jury Exhibit Two in evidence: 'I hereby certify that this is a true and complete copy of the original report,' signed in ink, Farouk . . . uh . . . Abaram. Last name spelled A-B-D-A-R-R-A-H-I-M."

"Abd ar-Rahim," murmured Winter reflexively.

"Reading from Exhibit Two in pertinent part: fourteen glassine envelopes containing white powder, cocaine present in each, net weight ten grams. Does the jury have any questions? Let the record show that there are no questions. Has the grand jury been charged on the law of sale and possession of a controlled substance? Let the record so indicate. That concludes the case against Manuel Vega. I will leave the exhibits with the foreman for your perusal and withdraw while you consider your findings."

The shuffle of the assistant district attorney, court stenographer, and grand jury warden leaving the room roused Winter and the rest of the jury from their collective torpor.

"Package deal. Open and shut. All the charges together. Let's vote." The adenoidal plea for instant hanging came from a pear-shaped man named Joe from the Chelsea neighborhood of Manhattan. Joe operated on the familiar theory that the State of New York, in its all-seeing benevolence, would never seek to prosecute an innocent person.

"Anyone wanna see the exhibits?" offered the square-jawed, Runyonesque foreman standing behind the bench and leaning against it with two papers in his hand. Silence. "Ready to vote?" Hands were already up. "All charges—third-degree sale, third-degree possession, seventh-degree possession—all together? All in favor?" With a languid gesture Winter joined the other twenty-two jurors in indicting Manuel Vega for selling ten grams of cocaine to an undercover police officer.

The jury secretary seated beside the foreman picked up a bell and tinkled it. The assistant district attorney hustled in officiously, grabbed his evidence and his indictment, gave a perfunctory nod to the citizens who had been compelled to endure his presentation, and swept grandly from the room. Passing him in the doorway was a fat, ill-kempt woman known to the jury from earlier cases. Her good-natured ability to move a case briskly along had earned her the jury's high estimation as the least unappealing assistant district attorney.

"If this is another three-three-seven, we quit!" whined Joe. Joe could whine and laugh at the same time. "No indictments for sales under fifty thousand dollars!"

"Good afternoon again. I'm Marie Keegan, assistant district attorney for New York County. I am going to present the People's case against"—she consulted a piece of paper on the lectern—"Raelene Montgomery. You will hear two witnesses, Police Officer Sandra Beeman and Detective Daryll Gregory, and then I will ask you to vote on a charge of sale of a controlled substance in the fifth degree and possession of a controlled substance in the fifth degree. Please call Police Officer Beeman."

The warden put down his newspaper and got up from his desk. He walked to the small door reserved for jury members and witnesses and shouted, "Beeman!"

"Fifth degree. It's either Valium or Darvon," whispered the curly-haired young man to Winter's right. "I just won't vote on those. I don't think it's right. Doctors give them away. I have some in my bag right now."

Winter settled his elbows into the indentations on the arms of the chair, considered fantasizing further about the woman in front of him, but instead shut his eyes and tuned out the testimony. He despised sailing with the blind passion of a person who had never sailed, but the closest thing he could imagine to serving on a special narcotics grand jury was being becalmed. Five days down, fourteen to go: neither special, nor grand, nor, given the 99+ percent indictment rate, jurylike, but nevertheless indubitably narcotic.

Twenty jurors had been assigned seats in the three rows of red leather chairs. The foreman, deputy foreman, and secretary sat facing them behind a long judicial bench of dark, scarred wood. To the jurors' left was a rickety lectern for the district attorneys, to their right a witness chair set into a niche in the bench. Behind the bench a warped and yellowed cardboard sign read: IN CASE OF EMERGENCY, OXYGEN EQUIPMENT IS LOCATED ON THE THIRD FLOOR. The New York State flag and a poster on the door to the corridor illustrating the Heimlich maneuver completed the room's decor.

It made no difference to Winter. From the very first day his fleeting moments of alertness had been increasingly and then obsessively occupied with the exotic, enticing head in front of him. To a man of Winter's generation, which had achieved worldly awareness just as the war against Ho Chi Minh was giving way to the war against Richard Nixon, demi-punk was an atrocity against the semi-hip styles of his youth. Worse yet, Pansy Garden—he had noted her name on the jury secretary's attendance chart—read lurid paperback romances in the jury waiting room during breaks. In Winter's view, women who elected to read about "urgent hardening desire" and "quivering dewy openness" on the Scottish moors or at Napoleon's court ranked with rock videos and computer games as threats to western civilization.

And yet . . . and yet the way the smooth curve of her long neck articulated with her delicate skull just behind her ears produced the most extraordinarily alluring soft bulges of smooth white skin. At times Winter could barely refrain from reaching out and touching them, or stroking her turbulent auburn mane.

Winter tuned back in to the last of the assistant district attorney's presentation. The Valium dealer was indicted by the time the door closed. The warden reentered to announce a ten-minute break before the next case.

Overheated and dingy like the jury room itself, the jurors' waiting room was also dark and narrow. It was furnished with a small metal table, four chairs, a coat rack, and an empty water cooler flanked by several dozen empty five-gallon water bottles. Winter half listened to Joe's whining discourse on why Chelsea wasn't like what Chelsea had used to be like before. Winter wasn't certain just where Chelsea was or when before was.

"Is your name *really* Castle Winter?"

Winter awoke and stared. Pansy Garden was slender and lithe and had clear green eyes and a bold alto voice that fit just right with her auburn hair. It struck Winter suddenly that he no longer noticed her dark purple—almost black—lipstick and nail polish. "Yes, it is," he replied. Such a fine head, he thought; such a fine body—such a pathetic mind.

"I think it's the most romantic name I've ever heard. I read a book once named *Castle Winter*. Have you read it?

There's this girl Audrey who comes to this great castle to tutor the children of a man who's lost his wife?"

"I haven't read it," said Winter hastily. "But you have a pretty good name yourself. It's Pansy Garden, isn't it?"

"You like it? I do. It used to be Audrey. Changing it changed my whole life. Names tell you about a person. You think so too, I know. Every time the district attorney reads one of those foreign chemist's names I can hear you say it over to yourself."

Winter flushed at the realization that Pansy Garden had been paying attention to him. "I'm just correcting the pronunciation," he said. "I don't know why, but almost everyone who does chemical analysis for the police has an Arabic name. They must come from Egypt or Pakistan or Lebanon or someplace. Have you noticed that? The ballistics lab people are all Smith or Jones, but not the chemists. And the DAs butcher the names. I used to study Arabic and some of those other languages, and I don't like to hear them mispronounced." Winter thought he sounded pompous.

Pansy Garden's green eyes became even more limpid. "Arabic! How thrilling!" Suddenly the tinkle of the bell summoned the jurors back to their seats.

Winter looked at the back of Pansy's head. It was cocked slightly to the right in an ineffably provocative manner. Head-cockers are always flirts, he thought. He couldn't recall her cocking her head at any previous time. To his surprise he discovered a condition of urgent hardening desire overtaking him. He quelled it by dousing himself in the cold water of Assistant District Attorney Oshinsky's presentation.

"Officer Jackson, would you please tell the ladies and gentlemen of the grand jury what happened at that time, place, and occasion."

A black undercover policeman with a shaved head wearing a *Ghostbusters* sweatshirt and a tiny gold earring was in the witness chair. "I approached J.D. Greencoat—that is, John Doe Greencoat—whom I later learned to be Sidney Monroe, and asked him if the fuel was out. He asked me what I was looking for. I said I wanted a gram of coke. He took me into the lobby of 562 where we were having a drug-related conversation when someone came into the lobby and said the police were coming. We both ran." Officer Jackson winked at the grand jury. "We went up the stairs and down a hall to apartment 3-B, which I later learned was rented to Estelle Marie Whitehead. J.D. Redhat, whom I later learned to be Thaddeus Monroe, opened the door and said, 'You shouldn't come in here. The cops will follow you.' We went into the kitchen. On the kitchen table was a triple-beam scale, some glassine envelopes, a roll of aluminum foil, and a violin. J.D. Redhat asked me what I was looking for, and I said a gram. The top of the violin was held on with a rubber band. It didn't have no strings. He pulled a plastic bag of white powder out of the violin and weighed out a gram. He wrapped it in foil and handed it to me. Then I handed him two hundred twenty dollars in prerecorded buy money and left the set and radioed my backup."

"And what did you do with the foil of white powder?" Assistant District Attorney Oshinsky had on a blue three-piece suit.

"I vouchered it at the two-six precinct."

"And did you ask for a laboratory report?"

"Yes, I did."

Oshinsky went through the ritual of entering the lab report in evidence. Winter hadn't a clue as to the chemist's national origin, but he repronounced and apparently corrected the exotic name anyway in a slightly louder murmur than usual. Pansy Garden cocked her head to the other side.

A witness from the backup team testified to the seizure of white powder, a violin, and the drug paraphernalia. Winter had better luck with the second chemist's report.

"I hereby certify," read Oshinsky, "that this is a complete and accurate copy of the original, signed Samir . . . Magreebi."

"Maghribi," said Winter loudly enough to be heard in the front row.

Oshinsky cast a quizzical glance in Winter's direction and then resumed. "Reading in pertinent part: eighty-three glassine envelopes, cocaine present in each; one jar containing lactose, no controlled substance present; one plastic bag containing white powder, cocaine present; one Alliance triple-beam scale; one violin with seven lines of Arabic writing on inside of backboard and white powder residue, no controlled substance found. Net weight of cocaine 2.41 ounces."

After the session, as Winter readied himself for the January slush and wind, Pansy Garden spoke to him again. "Wasn't that exciting about the Arabic writing in the violin? You must be thrilled!" Winter looked at her and considered remarking that nothing had "thrilled!" him since age eighteen . . . except the back of her head. Then he thought better of it. "It's a mystery, isn't it?" she went on. "How that Arabic writing got there? Inside the violin? What are you going to do about it?"

Winter sighed. Pansy's captivating qualities were not as apparent once they were tucked inside a calf-length, down-filled coat and a knit helmet-like hat in matching lavender. He decided on diplomacy. "Unfortunately, we aren't allowed to speak to witnesses or district attorneys after a case. Otherwise I might have pursued it."

"I guessed you were like that. That's why I did it for you." Winter looked into her naïve, green-eyed (but black-lipped) face. "I told the DA you were an Arabic teacher and asked him how you could get a look at the violin."

Winter was amazed. "Did he tell you? On the first day, I asked a DA where I could buy some coffee, and he gave me a stiff lecture on nonfraternization."

"Of course he told me. I took this course at the New School on body language. It changed my whole life. While I was asking him about the violin, I signaled very subtly with my body that I found him attractive and would be happy to have sex with him. Let's go to dinner. Or are you married?"

"Uh, divorced."

"Gay?"

"No."

"Good."

2

"Do you know why I picked you up?" Pansy plucked a red pepper from a glutinous dish of Hunan-style bean curd and popped it in her mouth. Winter winced. "Two reasons. First, because you're the handsomest man I have seen in three months, and second, because you have to sieze life. I do things like that, and they change my whole life. One day I tore off a postcard at the bottom of one of those ads in the subway. That was the beginning of my career in computing."

"You have a career in computing?" Winter couldn't remember having fewer opportunities to speak in a friendly conversation. Being laconic by nature, he didn't mind. Besides, Pansy's voice made words sound like crystal fresh water bubbling out of a spring, as long as Winter didn't attend too closely to their meaning.

"It was for a programming school. I took the course, and after that I got my job at Software City. I sell software, but my real talent is Beta-testing, debugging new programs that haven't been released. What kind of hardware do you have?"

Too old for punk, thought Winter smugly, but not too old to have a computer. "I have an Apple IIe."

"You should unload it for a Mac, if you want to stick with Apple, probably a Mac SE. The IIe is a fossil. What text adventures do you play?"

"What's a text adventure?"

Pansy lowered her head and stared at him with serious incredulity from beneath purple shadowed eyelids. "Text adventures, Castle, are life. By showing you an imaginary world, they show you the real world."

"Fine, but what are they?"

"Well, you boot the game and a description of some situation comes up. If you have a computer with good graphics, like a Mac, there are pictures with it. So, there you are in a spaceship, or a spooky cavern, or a castle, or something. Then it asks you what you intend to do: go some direction, take something, say something. As soon as you type in what you want to do—that's real easy, usually two or three words—you hit Return and find out what happens. If you go east, you get to the emerald lake where the grogs are lurking. If you go west, you fall off the cliff and die. That sort of thing. So you have adventures.

"So you want to know how that's like life? I always save the fried dumplings for last and pretend they're dessert. Desserts are terrible in Chinese restaurants." She wedged a dumpling between her straight, white teeth and guillotined it. "A text adventure," she continued when she had finished chewing, "is like life because nothing happens if you don't make choices. Simple choices. You just do it. You sieze your opportunity. Now take for example this Arab violin. What do I care about an Arab violin? Nothing. But you said the word Arabic; I want to get to know you; so I just did it. In text adventures you make decisions just to see what happens. I do something on the Arabic; I tell you; you ask me to dinner. It's bizarre, just like a text adventure."

"You asked me to dinner."

"Whatever. You know, you passed a guy on the street today who could have put you on the way to making a million bucks." Winter lifted his elegant eyebrows. "You had to ask him the right question, but you blew it. It's like in Zork III where you come upon this old man sleeping in one of the rooms. You type in 'Waken man,' and he wakes up. But nothing else works unless you've already gotten the bread from the cliff and offer it to him. If you do that, he points to the wall, and you see a secret door there you couldn't see before. It's all a matter of asking the right question or doing the right thing.

"You want to know why I wear my hair this way? Older guys like you always want to know why I wear my hair this way. It's not because it's punk looking. It's because I read this book about bumps on the skull. A hundred years ago skull bumps were very big. Like studying them was big, not the bumps. They called it phrenology. So this guy writes a new book on it. It changed my whole life. It said that these little bumps on your skull behind your ears here"—she touched the focal points of Winter's wilder fantasies—"cause men to get sexually aroused." Winter felt his face flush. "Castle, I'm telling you the truth! You think it's funny, but that's what it said! So a million girls would say that it's silly. But I say, so let me get my hair cut to show my bumps." Pansy slapped the table and laughed heartily. "That's text adventure!"

"Tell me about Software City," said Winter to change the subject.

Pansy winked at him. "You weren't born with the name Castle, were you. You took it. I can tell."

"No, I was born with it."

"My father is the son of a Basque immigrant who moved to Wyoming to herd sheep. Do you believe that?"

"Your voice doesn't sound like Wyoming."

"What did kids call you when you were little?"

Winter opened his mouth but said nothing.

"Come on, what did they call you?"

"Johnny."

"That's it, isn't it? Your real name. John Winter. I can see why you changed it."

"I like the name John Winter. John Castle Winter. Has a nice ring to it. Castle's my mother's maiden name. It's really my middle name."

"Tell me about when you decided to drop the John."

"My former wife, Judith, talked me into it. It's an interesting story."

"Tell me while we walk to the subway." Pansy stood up abruptly and started to wrestle with her down coat. "What do you do for a living, Castle?"

"I do real estate analysis for an insurance company."

"Then dinner's on me. I probably make more than you do. You should find a career in computing. It's changed my whole life." Winter trailed her between tables to the front of the restaurant, deflecting her dangling coat sleeve from a hot-and-sour-soup tureen and then from a gruesome brown dish of sea slugs.

"Thank you for dinner," said Winter as they set off through the chill toward the subway. "What I was going to say about my name is that when I got married, I was a graduate student studying Arabic and Persian. But my then-wife Judith made me realize that there wasn't a chance in a million that I would ever make it as a professor. I wasn't dynamic enough. And even if I did, it would probably be at Boise State, and we'd be stuck there for life. The job market for professors was just terrible. Anyway, she said I should cash in my chips and take a course designed to turn Ph.D. students into businessmen. And she thought if I was going into business, I should have a more distinctive name. So that was when I switched from John to Castle. I took the course and got the job I have now."

"I wouldn't call that an interesting story," said Pansy reflectively. "Why did you get a divorce?"

"Judith left me."

"That sounds like an interesting story."

"It's also a private one."

Pansy was unfazed. "I go uptown here. I'll see you tomorrow at the jury. We never did get around to talking about the violin, you know. But we can work on that tomorrow."

"Actually, I don't really care about the violin."

"The Arab violin? Of course you do. Why else do you think I virtually offered myself to that sleazy DA? That's what we went to dinner about, remember? I'm going to show you how to sieze control of your life, Castle. I'm going to turn your life into a text adventure."

Winter grabbed her upper arm and drew in a breath. "I already know how to sieze control of my life, Pansy. Try this." He cleared his throat. "Why don't you come on home with me and spend the night? We can talk about the violin all you want and make sweet music together."

Pansy smiled sweetly with her purple-black lips. "Heavens no, Castle. Don't be silly. You're incredibly handsome, but up close you smell like butter. Did you know that? I'm a vegetarian. I can't stand sex with men who smell like butter. It comes from eating meat fat. I read a book about it. It changed my whole life." She skipped down the Uptown steps and disappeared.

3

Pansy Garden telephoned Castle Winter the next morning. She told him how to get to the office of Samir Maghribi. At the police station she borrowed twenty dollars from him.

Mr. Maghribi, the police chemist, was Egyptian. He was also an official. He sat behind a gray steel desk and a yellow bronze nameplate. His physique was the outcome of five thousand years of genetic adaptation among Egyptian officials making them peculiarly suited to sitting: very big on the bottom and in the midsection; torso tapering upward to narrow, sloping shoulders; fatty jowls concealing a presumed neck; and a somewhat conical cranium topped by closely trimmed curly black hair—a figure, thought Winter as he stood behind Pansy in the small, featureless office, that would probably evolve further, over the next five millenia, into a perfect organic pyramid.

The view from Mr. Maghribi's side of the desk was no less jaundiced. Pansy Garden was an attractive young woman, but Mr. Maghribi did not like the combination of purple-black lips, green eyes, and auburn hair. It reminded him of certain severe and revolting toxicological symptoms. This was the woman, he thought, that Assistant District Attorney Oshinsky insisted he speak to? And the darkly handsome but strangely apathetic looking gentleman at her side, this was the purported distinguished professor of Arabic? Mr.

Maghribi was by training a scientist and a skeptic. He was also, by bureaucratic tradition, inclined to be unhelpful and dilatory unless persuaded that it was not in his interest.

Pansy Garden turned him around in forty-five seconds flat, not counting preliminary introductions. "Mr. Maghribi, I believe in fate. Don't you?" Her voice was languid, even seductive, as she slipped into the straight chair on the supplicant's side of the desk. Her crystal-pure gaze found his tiny brown eyes in the depths of their fat-shrouded sockets. "Not one chemist in a million would have mentioned seven lines of Arabic in his report, and not one grand jury in a thousand would have had on it an Arabic professor with a special interest in violin messages. But fate does not work alone!" she gushed theatrically, leaning across the desk and passionately clasping one of Mr. Maghribi's pudgy hands in her own. Mr. Maghribi swayed backward in his chair but quickly regained his equilibrium like a ballasted balloon toy righting itself after a child's punch.

"Please, Miss Garden." He carefully extracted his hand from her grasp and hid it from further assault under the desk. "My understanding is that you and Professor Winter have an interest in the violin with the Arabic writing. I have here a photograph of it." He withdrew an eight-by-ten black-and-white glossy print from the middle drawer of his desk and passed it to Pansy, who handed it to Winter.

Winter's heart pounded. He scowled. The picture showed the inside of a violin with the top removed. Written on the backboard were seven lines of Arabic script, alternating short with long. He couldn't read a single word. His perfectly shaped and elegantly arched right eyebrow, which twitched occasionally even when he was relaxed, made several dramatic efforts to jump into his sculptured black hairline. "Pencil?"

"Yes."

"Very interesting."

"Curious, don't you think?" Mr. Maghribi's voice sounded doubtful.

Winter took a bold decision. "Not Arabic, of course."

"Of course," agreed Mr. Maghribi.

Winter sighed inwardly as the hook slipped loose from his flesh. If an educated Arab agreed that the language wasn't Arabic, assuming Pansy hadn't made any other linguistic claims for him, he was home free. "Fact of the matter is, I can't read a single word."

"That's what is so curious," agreed Mr. Maghribi, actually seeming to take an interest in the problem. "I can see the name Muhammad in line five, of course"—Winter nodded—"but nothing else means anything to me. My first thought was that a child had written it, but how do you write on the inside of a violin? And you see these smears?" He pointed to some blurred letters in line three and a bit farther on to some letters covered with a dark blot. "Glue on top of the letters. So the writing must have been done before the violin was put together, unless the glue is from a repair."

"That's very curious," said Winter with genuine puzzlement. "Perhaps we can examine the violin itself. It might have some identifying marks on it."

Mr. Maghribi glanced at Pansy. Pansy looked away. "Unfortunately, it must be kept in the property room until the district attorney decides he doesn't need it as evidence. Then it goes back to its owner."

"Oh. Who's the owner?" asked Winter.

Mr. Maghribi glanced again at Pansy. "The Superintendant of Properties told me there had been a report from one M. Mustafa about a stolen violin with writing in it. I might be able to find out more," he ventured, "but I'm not really supposed to give out that sort of information."

"Of course not," said Winter. "I wouldn't dream of asking. Besides, since the alphabet is Arabic but the language isn't, it doesn't actually fit my research on . . . uh . . . Arabic violin inscriptions." Mr. Maghribi looked crestfallen. "But I would like to keep this photograph. If it's an extra print," Winter added hurriedly. "All violin inscriptions interest me somewhat. It's just that right now I'm working only on ones in Arabic."

Mr. Maghribi looked at Pansy, who shrugged charmingly.

"I'm sorry, Professor Winter. The photograph is police property."

There being nothing more to say, the three of them burst simultaneously into an abrupt and awkward leave-taking. As they walked the short distance from the police station to the courthouse for the afternoon jury session, Winter confronted Pansy. "I don't understand it. When we walked into that office, everything about that man said that he wasn't going to be helpful and that he was going to use a hundred and fifty rules to avoid telling us anything. A minute later, zip!—out comes a photograph we haven't even gotten around to asking for. I just don't see how you do it. You wrap men around your little finger in ways I can't even begin to grasp. It's simply amazing. I suppose you read some book about how to use your eyes or your voice and it changed your whole life."

"I slipped him the twenty bucks when I reached for his hand."

"Oh." Winter fell silent. Pansy had nothing more to say.

They walked to the subway together after a hot, tedious four hours during which the twenty-three grand jurors, supported by their warden and stenographer, indicted six poor, uneducated, and unemployable New Yorkers on the testimony of ten police witnesses as marshalled by five different assistant district attorneys.

"The case against Sidney and Thaddeus Monroe has been dropped. They're cooperating with the DA," said Pansy.

"Who are Sidney and Thaddeus Monroe?"

"J.D. Redhat and J.D. Greencoat."

"Were they the ones who said they had found the loaded shotgun on the street and had just put it in their closet for safekeeping?"

"No. Don't you remember? J.D. Greencoat took an undercover cop up to J.D. Redhat's apartment, and that's where the violin was found. The case has been dropped so the violin isn't needed for evidence. So we can get to see it."

"Not if that M. Mustafa who phoned in about it picks it up right away. What do we want to see it for, anyway? I can't read a word of it."

They had reached a slushy streetcorner when Pansy stopped. "If this were a text adventure, Castle, you would come to a room, and the description of it would say, 'There is a violin visible.' You would type in 'Take violin' and hit Return. Then it would say 'Taken.' Then you would type in, maybe, 'Play violin,' and it would say something wise-ass like 'You're not Pavarotti'—"

"Paganini."

"Whatever. Then you would type in 'Open violin.'"

"Why would I type that?"

"Because that's the whole idea. You try things and see what works. So you type in 'Open violin,' and it says 'You take off the top of the violin and find seven lines of Arabic script written in pencil on the inside of the backboard.' Then you type 'Read Arabic script,' and it says, 'It is in an unknown language.' Then what? You don't just stop there, Castle. Surely you can see that. There's something you can do that will tell you what language it is. That's the nature of the game. That's what we work on next."

"Pansy," said Winter seriously, "life is not a game, much less a text adventure."

"Did your former wife Judith divorce you for being a wimp?" She glanced toward the traffic. "I've got to run." She gave him a quick kiss on the lips. He felt the cold tip of her nose brush his cheek. As she turned toward the street, a green BMW paused at the curb. The door opened, and Assistant District Attorney Oshinsky beckoned Pansy inside. In a moment she was gone.

Winter stood in the slush and pondered the word "wimp." Judith had preferred "ineffectual." She was more literary, sometimes even pretentious, in her expression. Perhaps it was to make up for not having gone to college. Her favorite way of describing their separation was to quote Eleanor of Aquitaine's remark to her husband, King Louis VII: "Why do I renounce you? Because of your fecklessness. You are not worth a rotten pear."

4

Frankie was short, slender, and fourteen. He had yellowish brown skin and short, tightly curled hair. He couldn't remember Santo Domingo, where he'd been born. Deliveries and odd jobs for Software City usually didn't call upon his natural intelligence and cleverness, but any job at all was more than most of his friends had. On the streets Frankie had already seen most of what life had to offer and had reserved comment.

Frankie was much too wise to ask questions when Pansy Garden intercepted him on his way to work and hustled him onto the subway. But as her voice bored persuasively into his ear over the screech and rumble of the downtown local, questions nevertheless came to mind: Why did he have to pretend to the police that he was Pansy's son? Why did she have on such ugly clothes—plain, buttoned-up trench coat; gray scarf pulled tight around her face; round, goggly glasses; and *no* lipstick? Why did the fake-looking ID card she handed him have the name Maryam Mustafa on it? Work itself out, thought Frankie.

By the time they got to the precinct house, he had his speech down, even though it still didn't make sense. Pansy took a seat on a molded plastic chair bolted to the wall opposite the high counter. She put the Macy's bag she was carrying on the floor beside her. Frankie was barely tall enough to engage the attention of the bosomy, blue-uniformed policewoman riffling through papers behind the counter. "My name is Abdul Mustafa," he said softly with his heavy Dominican intonation. "That is my mama over there. She can't talk English. Her name is Maryam Mustafa. This is her card." He pushed the card with Maryam Mustafa's name on it across the counter. "She wants to get her violin. It was stolen. She got a call saying she could come get it."

The policewoman looked at him dully. "Take a seat. Fill this out." She pushed a flimsy white form marked PROPERTY VOUCHER/RECEIPT back across the counter.

Frankie took the seat beside Pansy. He looked around as she filled out the form. The street door opened and a bearded black man entered. He was well over six feet tall and wore a white ankle-length gown, black wing tip shoes, a black overcoat, and a white knitted skullcap. A string of red plastic prayer beads with a fluffy gold tassel dangled from his hand.

"Muhammad Mustafa, Officer. Here for my violin," he said to the policewoman.

Without looking up she pushed the white form across the counter. "Over there. Fill it out. You'll be called."

Pansy fixed the imposing man with her best Islamic revolutionary scowl. He looked back at her with evident surprise and curiosity, then turned to completing the form. Frankie looked around to check out the emergency exits. A glass-paneled door behind the policewoman seemed to connect with the rest of the police station. To the right of the counter was a corridor with several other doors. None was marked EXIT.

Five minutes passed. The front door opened again and a fat black woman with broad lips and nose swept in from the cold. She was dressed in what Pansy took to be African finery under an open winter coat—a voluminous bright yellow flowered gown and a floppy crownlike turban made from the same cloth. She announced herself to the policewoman as Mamadou Mustafa come to claim her stolen violin. She and the bearded man exchanged venomous scowls as she sat down. She quickly filled out the white form and got up and slapped it back on the counter.

"We best be goin'," whispered Frankie in Pansy's ear.

"They're fakes," she whispered back.

"So we," replied Frankie. "But they look like the kind of people got more friends than we got."

The glass-paneled door behind the counter opened, and someone handed the policewoman a plastic bag. She pulled a violin out of the bag. "Mustafa, M.," she read from a tag attached to its neck. Red rubber bands held the stringless instrument together at its waist.

The white-gowned man and the yellow-gowned woman stepped to the counter. Pansy prodded Frankie forward. Frankie was a foot and a half shorter than the man and a hundred and fifty pounds lighter than either of them.

"Gimme my violin," commanded the woman. "I'm Mamadou Mustafa. It's my violin." The man maintained a more dignified, but nevertheless intimidating, demeanor waiting for his presence to be recognized. Frankie held back, scarcely visible from across the counter. Suddenly two men issued from behind the glass-paneled door and conferred with the policewoman. Pansy immediately recognized the heavy, pear-shaped form of Samir Maghribi and turned her head to look out the window at the slushy street corner. The reflection in the glass allowed her to watch the heavyset uniformed officer with Maghribi consult with the policewoman.

"Well, we seem to have three M. Mustafas here, all wanting their violin." The surprisingly lilting voice was that of the officer who had just entered. "What's the story, Muhammad?"

The bearded man had a sonorous baritone voice. "My violin was stolen. It had Arabic in it. If that's it, I want it back. It's special. I don't know who these other dudes are."

"Ain't your violin! It's my violin! Been stolen once. You ain't gonna steal it again." The yellow-swathed woman was steamed up and ready to fight.

"All right, hold it down," said the officer. "Who's the third Mustafa?"

"My mother . . . sir," said Frankie softly. "That's her over there. She don't speak English. It's her violin."

The officer, who had a cheerful, ruddy, Irish face, appeared to be enjoying himself. "Well now, I telephoned M. Mustafa yesterday to tell him he could pick up his property this morning, but his number had been disconnected. As I recollect, however, he had a sort of stutter in his voice when he first reported the violin being missing. I don't think any of you M. Mustafas sounds like him at all."

"My husband, Arnold Muhammad Mustafa," declared the African-looking woman promptly. "He died."

"My half-brother," intoned the tall man.

"My father?" said Frankie softly, glancing back at Pansy, who still had her face averted.

"Your father?" queried the officer.

"Uncle?" offered Frankie hopefully.

The officer grinned and winked. "Fact of the matter is, none of you has presented any photo-identification. On the other hand, the man with the stutter hasn't shown up either. So whose violin is it going to be? This officer here"—he inclined his head toward Mr. Maghribi—"knows what's written inside it. Let's see if any of you do. How about you, Sister?"

Mamadou Mustafa seemed hesitant for the first time. "It's my husband's name and address in Nigeria," she ventured. "But I can't read it myself. He come from a different part of the country."

"Very different I would imagine," said the officer. "What's your version, Muhammad?"

The white-robed black man did not hesitate. "*Allahu akbar. Allahu akbar. La ilaha illa Allah wa Muhammad rasul Allah,*" he intoned grandly. "That means 'God is great. God is great. There's no God but Allah. Muhammad is Allah's messenger.'"

The jovial officer nodded and looked impressed. Then he turned to Frankie. Frankie retreated to the chairs, held a whispered conference with Pansy, and returned. "My mom says she can't read it. But she says it isn't in Arabic. It's just in that alphabet. Don't ask me what that means. She also says that it's seven lines long, and line five has the name Muhammad."

Mr. Maghribi pulled the officer back toward the glass-paneled door and engaged him in conversation. Then Mr. Maghribi departed through the door. The ruddy-faced officer came back to the counter. "The prize goes to you," he said to Frankie. "Your mother has to sign for it. Can she do that?" Pansy had already gotten up and approached the counter. "I thought you couldn't speak English, Mrs. Mustafa? How did you know what I was saying?"

Pansy scowled. "I speak English," she said in what she hoped was a weird enough accent. "My religion forbids me to speak to unbelievers and men. I will have to wash four times for speaking to you. It is worse than speaking to pig." Frankie stared fixedly at the floor. He wished Pansy hadn't added the last sentence. The tall black man and the African woman looked at both of them with malice but edged away from the counter. Pansy signed the receipt in a loopy scrawl and put the violin in her shopping bag. Then she leaned over and whispered in Frankie's ear.

"My mama want to know if there's a ladies' room," said Frankie.

The policewoman, who had continued to riffle through papers and ignore the proceedings around her, said reflexively, "Down the hall, second door on the left."

Frankie looked out the station window as he waited for Pansy to return from the ladies' room. The bearded man was loitering outdoors at the corner to the left of the station's entrance. The fat woman was standing by a car halfway down the block in the other direction talking through the window to a black man with a high flat-top haircut in the front passenger's seat.

Pansy strode past Frankie without looking at him and skipped out of the building. The glasses were gone, and her semi-punk auburn hair was gloriously unscarfed. Her lips were their familiar dark purple. The beige trench coat had disappeared into the shopping bag with the violin and been replaced by her lavender down coat. The Macy's bag itself was encased within a Bloomingdale's bag that had previously been folded inside it. With her head in the air she breezed past the African-looking woman and turned the corner.

Five minutes later Mamadou Mustafa reentered the station. "Where's you mama?" she said to Frankie. "She takin' a awful long time peein'."

"Gone," replied Frankie. "Back door."

"What about you?" The woman looked ominous.

"Waiting for a cab."

"What cab?"

"Mama said she gonna send a cab. Didn't want me going home alone. Safety."

The woman lowered her voice and spoke with hate-filled intensity. "You tell your mama that she steal hundred thousand dollars from us she get in a whole lotta trouble."

"My cab now," said Frankie, brushing past the angry woman. He darted out of the building and into the yellow taxi that had just pulled up. He gave a frightened look out the back window as the cab pulled into the traffic, but he couldn't tell if anyone was following.

"A hundred thousand dollars," he said to himself.

Pansy presented the violin to Castle Winter after the grand jury had finished its soporific deliberations for the day. She explained it as an unauthorized loan made possible because Mr. Maghribi was such a sweetie. They took a cab together to Castle's apartment on West 108th Street. Ordinarily Castle would have been agitated over whether his bachelor mess might offend a female guest, and Pansy would have been intent upon finding clues to the microcosm and the macrocosm in the disposition of a gentleman friend's personal effects. But in truth, excitement and curiosity about the violin had overcome them both and pushed all other considerations to the back of their minds.

A minute examination of the violin yielded no new information. There was no label or stamp or written mark anywhere aside from the seven lines of script inside. Nor was the instrument in any way exceptional as a violin. It was sort of old looking, and the finish wasn't very nice, but it was otherwise, as far as they could determine, a most ordinary violin.

"A violin has four strings, doesn't it," said Pansy, looking at the four tuning pegs at the end of the neck.

"One goes around each of those pegs. You turn the peg to tighten the string and change the pitch."

"And these little grooves on this bump of wood here are what the strings go over?"

"Right," replied Castle. "That little bump is called the 'nut.'" He was proud of himself for remembering the word from a crossword puzzle. "It's like a fret on a guitar except that a violin doesn't have frets."

"This one has five grooves."

"It does?"

"Yeah. Look. Four and then a fifth one right next to the one on the end."

"Looks like a mistake," said Castle, examining the end of the violin's neck. "There are only four pegs so there couldn't have been five strings. I think whoever made it filed a groove in the wrong place and then corrected it by filing a new one next to it. There's only about a sixteenth of an inch between them."

The telephone rang. It was for Pansy.

"Hi, Frankie. You were really great. I mean super." Castle listened closely while resting his eyes idly on the inscription in the violin. All of the potentialities of having a sexually alluring single woman visit his apartment flooded suddenly into his mind.

"How'd you know where I was?" continued Pansy. There was a long pause. "Why did you do that?" Another long pause. "A hundred thousand dollars? Fantastic! Take care of yourself, Frankie. I'll see you soon. It's sweet of you to take care of me." She hung up.

"Who's Frankie?"

"A friend who helped me get the violin."

"He's that assistant district attorney, isn't he?"

"No."

"Yes he is. I'm not a dummy, Pansy. You couldn't have just gone down and borrowed this from the police the way you said you did. You had to know what to do. And who was able to tell you? The DA. What's his name? Frank Oshinsky, isn't it? The one you told by body language that you wanted to sleep with him? Remember? He picked you up on the corner last night in a goddamn BMW, and this morning you know all about how to claim this goddamn violin from the police. He just has a lot of nerve to call you here. That's all I can say."

"You're getting hysterical, Castle. I'm not going to talk to you about this."

"You spent the night with him last night, didn't you? I'm not criticizing. I just want a straight answer. I smell like butter, but you hop into bed with a DA just to get your hands on a silly violin."

"He's a vegetarian, and his name is David."

"So you don't deny it."

"Why should I?"

Castle stopped. He found he couldn't think of a single good reason why Pansy Garden shouldn't do whatever she wanted with whomever she fancied. "I'm sorry, Pansy," he said, suddenly contrite. "You're right. I was getting hysterical. Just for a moment it seemed like I was married again and I had some sort of claim on you. It's hard to go from being married to being unmarried, you know. I haven't seen very many women since Judith left."

"I'm not surprised." Pansy gave her auburn mane a shake. "But hey, forget it. What Frankie said on the phone is that this violin is worth a hundred thousand dollars. He also said some people are real anxious to get it, and he thinks I shouldn't go home tonight. Just in case they've figured out who has it."

Castle looked astonished. "This crumby violin worth a

hundred thousand? I don't believe it. If it's worth so much, why didn't the DA tell you last night? Why did he let you borrow it?"

"The DA is David Oshinsky," explained Pansy patiently. "He's a very nice and quite virile man with a great future ahead of him. The person on the phone was Frankie. David doesn't know the violin is worth money."

"Then don't tell me who Frankie is. Please. I don't want to get involved in your personal life. We're friends. You have your friends, and I have mine. And I smell like butter. So that's that."

"Right. Whatever."

"Tomorrow we'll take the violin to a violin store and get it appraised."

"Castle, I don't think that's a good idea. I think we should keep it here. From what Frankie said, maybe it's worth a lot of money to certain people for some reason other than being a musical instrument."

"I don't get it."

"Neither do I."

"The violin will have to be returned to the police."

They sat for a long while in silence looking at nothing. Eventually Pansy said, "What have you got to eat?"

"Let's look in the fridge."

They ate lettuce, tomato, and mayonnaise sandwiches. Castle longed to fry up some bacon but restrained himself. He didn't know how long it took for a butter smell to dissipate from the human body, but he had to start sometime.

They agreed that Castle would take a vacation day from the grand jury and try to get the violin inscription translated. Castle offered Pansy his bed, but she opted for the floor. A book on spinal cord consciousness, it seemed, had changed her whole life.

5

Fear was Castle Winter's strongest memory of Columbia University. His three years as a graduate student in Middle Eastern languages were almost two decades behind him, but the old apprehensive feelings seemed to regain life from the campus's red brick buildings like ivy turning green in the spring. Castle opened the heavy wooden door of Kent Hall a gainfully employed private person on a legitimate quest for expert knowledge. Two steps inside and he was again a cowering graduate student, an untutored acolyte at the altar of exotic learning, a cringing slave to every strange professorial whim.

Professor Grete Weisspferd greeted him with her familiar all-purpose smile and seemed vaguely to remember him. To Castle's surprise, Professor Weisspferd had aged in twenty years. He suddenly realized that he remembered his professors as petrified intellectual gargoyles rather than biological organisms. She was still tall and angular, but her shoulders were rounded, her straw-colored hair gone partly to gray. Yet the voice remained: a small, musical, German voice articulated at the front of the mouth as if she were nibbling on the words. The memory awakened of Professor Weisspferd's spiritual resonance with the mystic Sufi poetry of Islam, her habit of lecturing with her eyes delicately closed, and the occasional glimpses she allowed, through the veil of her gentleness, of the steely Teutonic mind lurking behind it.

Professor Weisspferd spoke Arabic, Turkish, Persian, Urdu, Punjabi, and Sindhi. Castle presented her with his meticulously drawn copy of the violin message:

1 ھو لل ھائ سلا و فع

2 ھج لو لکفتو ھیب بٹ الکوٰ خت بش کتد بش ساٰبع شفر فج لبا

3 ساٰنٲو ـ ـ تں کبا لکا   *hard to read*

4 فنعٰ کو فنع مٯ دٯ سیر کٯ سں لٹبا کٯر ممونا بسرت فنع مٯ ـ   *glue*

5 ککں سں مو محمد ککسں [ر] → ؟ →   *hard to read* →

6 سرکو ممو ٹں سں ٹغ برٹ دو عنا عل کل کل عل لا للا ـ [ ] ؟

7 سلم لل سو للا   *copied by J. Castle Winter*

"No," she said slowly after a long look, "it isn't any of those. I see the name Muhammad, but nothing else means anything. It's too bad. When you showed it to me and told me it was from a violin, I was reminded of the wonderful old Sufi legend that Pir Muhammad Pahlavan wrote mystic words in his oud"—her eyes drifted shut; her fingers drew mystic letters in the air—"so that his disciples would find union with Allah when they danced to the music he played."

Professor Ihor Tretiak was round of face, thick of body, and nearly bald. His smile was sunshine. His high-pitched Ukrainian voice, which had come to English already permanently attuned to German and Turkish, was frequently impossible to understand. Besides Arabic, Persian, and the common

West European and Slavic languages, he knew Turkish, Azeri, Turkmen, Uzbek, Chuvash, Chagatay, Khirgiz, Uighur, and Kazakh, as well as a number of the less common Turkic languages.

"*Ja, ja.* Also. Is not, so to say, any Turkic, so to say, language. Of course, not Arabic or Persian. Could be, so to say, from Africa or India. You should ask Professor Weisspferd."

Castle had introduced the conversation by saying that Professor Weisspferd had referred him to Professor Tretiak. He ended it by thanking the great scholar for his helpful opinion. Professor Tretiak obviously had no recollection that he had ever seen Castle before, much less had him in class for two years.

Professor Robert Broyle carried into his sixties the tall, rangy physique of the epée fencer he had once been as a student in Germany. It was there he had learned to contain his naturally inquisitive and far-ranging American mind in the elastic truss of Oriental philology. The subsequent unpredictable hernias of his imagination suddenly breaking free had made him, for Castle, a most unforgettable professor.

"Nice to see you again, John. Ahah. Twenty years. What have you been up to?"

"I'm in real estate analysis."

"Ahah. Very interesting." Nothing in Broyle's voice supported the claim of interest. He looked at the paper in Castle's hand. "What do you have there?" Castle handed it to him. "Ahah."

Fifteen minutes and several dozen "ahahs" later, eight of the languages ruled out by Professors Weisspferd and Tretiak had again been eliminated from consideration, along with Kurdish, Pushtu, Borushaski, Tajik, Armenian, and the entire family of Dardic languages. Castle gathered from Broyle's mutterings that the Dardic languages were spoken by the descendants of several dozen families who had gotten lost in the mountains of eastern Afghanistan in 2000 B.C. and simply settled down when they couldn't find a trail out.

"Ahah. Now it could be from the Caucasus," Broyle mused. "There are a lot of languages there, and some of them have been written in Arabic script."

"Whom would I see?" asked Castle because it seemed to be the question Broyle was waiting to answer.

Castle retraced his steps along the wide, dingy hall and re-entered, after an annoyingly long wait, the clanking tomblike elevator he had arrived in. He descended safely.

As Professor Broyle had predicted, Castle found Jonathan Siracusa in the richly furbished East Asian library on the main floor of Kent Hall. He was working on his Japanese. He looked about twenty-five. He looked, in fact, just like the battalion of cut-throat young businessmen whom Castle often imagined were creeping up on him in deceptively peaceful disguise like warlike extras from the last act of Macbeth.

Broyle had described Siracusa as a graduate student with "a real way with languages." Castle himself had never had "a real way with languages." Siracusa scanned Castle's violin message and actually chuckled as he dismissed Georgian, Lezgi, Chechen, Abkhaz, Ossetic, and several lesser tongues from the list of possible languages. Castle recalled that as a graduate student he had commonly felt one other emotion besides fear: hatred for people who had "a real way with languages."

Mamadou Mustafa, looking hefty and mean, intercepted Pansy Garden a block from Software City and spoke to her in the colorful language of the people who accost pedestrians in New York City. "Whe' you goin'? You got my fuckin' violin. You give it to me, or there gonna be one dead white woman. I ain't shittin' you, honey. That violin worth a lotta money. Ten seconds you hand it over."

"Loved your yellow dress at the police station," said Pansy disarmingly. "It was so right." She reached into the plastic Bloomingdale's bag dangling from her left hand and pulled out a violin held together by thick red rubber bands. Holding the bag under her arm, she used both hands to slide aside the top of the instrument revealing the writing inside. Then she placed it in the thick, hard hands of Mamadou Mustafa. "Have a nice day," she said as she walked away.

A week of diligent research passed.

"How many languages do we have left?" said Pansy's voice through the receiver.

"I got a letter from Professor Isaac Ephraim at Harvard, a friend of Professor Broyle's." Castle wedged the telephone between his shoulder and his jaw and opened the envelope. "It says, 'Dear Mr. Winter,' blah, blah, blah, 'I have consulted my friend and colleague,' blah, blah, blah, 'and the conclusion has been reached that the language *is not*'—'is not' underlined—'Hausa, Fulani, Swahili, Wolof, or Kanuri.' Blah, blah, blah, 'suggests that it may be a Mandara derivative but is of the opinion that the letters are not *"ajami"* and not from West Africa. He also has a suspicion that the language may be Uiguric or an Eastern Turkic language.' Uiguric and Eastern Turkic languages are already out, so this leaves us with just about nothing."

"What's a Mandara derivative?"

"I haven't the foggiest idea." Castle reread the letter. "I'm very disappointed. I really thought the handwriting looked like some of the things in Hausa I found in the library."

"What's left?"

"Gypsy and Albanian, but I still haven't found an example of either of them in Arabic script. Anyway, I don't think it's Albanian because *Teach Yourself Albanian* shows a lot of suffixes that all look the same, and none of them show up in the violin."

"Wasn't Old Malay a possibility?"

"A professor named Raaf says it's not Old Malay."

"And then there was something else. You saw another handwriting that looked possible."

"Moro. Southern Philippines. The Met had a Koran from there that in the shape of the letters looked similar. I don't know where I might locate a Filipino Muslim who can read the old script, though. The Philippines UN mission hasn't answered my letter."

"Well?"

"Well what?"

"Well, what are you going to do next?"

"Call it quits. The owner probably has the violin back by now, anyway, and we'll never see it again."

A pregnant silence.

"You did return the violin to the police, didn't you, Pansy?"

Another silence, then, "Of course, Castle."

An aluminum tub of potato salad, a round plastic tray of sliced meat and cheese, a loaf of rye bread, a loaf of wheat bread, and a plastic dish of brownish mustard were more than the narrow metal table in the grand jury waiting room could hold. This became apparent when the overly energetic thrust of a plastic knife sent the mustard dish splatting to the floor.

The twenty-three grand jurors, crowded into the small, overheated room for a picnic celebrating their final day of service, condemned in one voice the inadequate table as if it had been caught selling syringes and glassine envelopes of dope. Miraculously only Castle Winter was standing near enough the splatter to receive a long ochre tendril of mustard across his shoe and trouser cuff.

The conversation that had died on the telephone the day before was resumed by Pansy and Castle around a protruding porcelain water fountain in the echoing courthouse corridor. Castle listened and scrubbed at his cuff with a sodden wad of paper napkins.

"Each of us will embark on a quest. You to find a Filipino

Muslim who can read his language in Arabic letters, I to discover the true identity of the M. Mustafa who reported the violin stolen. If the language is not Moro, we will go to Mr. Mustafa and ask him about it directly."

The mustard was exhibiting remarkable dyeing power.

"You may embark on whatever quest you like. I am quitting. The violin is back with the police. You may have my copy of the message. I am bored. This whole business is stupid." Castle's sentences followed the angry rhythm of his hand scouring his cuff. He was leaning over and standing on one leg, hopping occasionally to keep his balance. The exertion had brought the blood to his perfectly defined cheekline. His right eyebrow jerked uncontrollably.

"Anger interferes with communication," remarked Pansy.

Castle put his second foot on the ground and straightened up. "'Embark on a quest' is an adolescent, romantic phrase meaning 'do something stupid.' In this case, it means that I run around New York idiotically interrogating octogenarian Filipinos, and you snuggle into bed with 'quite virile' David Oshinsky and get him to tell you things he isn't supposed to tell you." He washed his fingers in the stream of water jetting upward from the fountain.

"Okay. We can quit out of this program if you don't want to play. There's no need to quarrel on our last day." Pansy shook her auburn hair and cocked her head at Castle.

"I thought I might drop by Software City next week and—"

"I'm not sure I'll be there."

Castle stopped abruptly. "Oh?" He felt ineffectual.

Pansy glanced at his damp hands. "Did you know that you can tell the size of a man's genitals from the length of his fingers? I read it in a book once."

Castle thrust his long-fingered hands angrily into his pockets. "This is what you do, isn't it, Pansy? You just blatantly use sex to get men to do what you want. A week ago you told me I smelled like butter so you couldn't sleep with me, and now you have the temerity to . . . to . . ."

"You don't smell quite so much like butter anymore, and I do find you incredibly handsome."

". . . hint that if I 'embark on a quest' with you, which means you sleeping with David Oshinsky, you might bestow some of your sexual favors on me."

"If that's the way you see things, Castle."

"I am not ineffectual!"

"Of course not. Ineffectual men don't scream and attract attention in courthouse corridors."

Castle looked around. Several clusters of people elsewhere in the hallway resumed their conversations. He trailed Pansy back to the door of the grand jury waiting room. "I will not embark on a quest," he whispered in her ear as they passed through the door. His lips almost brushed the sweet bulge of white skin behind her ear. Her hair smelled clean and enticing.

Castle sank into a reverie as an assistant district attorney presented the people's case against a doctor accused of illegally prescribing controlled substances. Judith had once noted the correspondence between the length of his fingers and of his other extremities. Castle had acted flattered—though why should he be flattered by the observation of a simple, if impressive, fact? . . . only to discover that Judith was setting him up.

"Remember that scene in Woody Allen's *Everything You Always Wanted to Know About Sex* where he's parodying Antonioni? Woody Allen thrusts his forearm up with his fist clenched and says 'like French bread,' *come il pane francese?*" She imitated the gesture. "With you, Castle, it's *come il pane americano—molto grande ma molle; s'il é duro, é disgustoso.*"

Big but soft. Unfair. Untrue. Moreover, Judith's Italian was bad. But she had cared enough to think the insult up.

Castle did not want to be feckless, or ineffectual . . . or unattached.

6

From an encyclopedia Castle learned that there were, or had been when the book was researched, between one and two million Muslims, popularly known as Moros, in the Philippines. Driven by a total and increasingly unbearable cutoff in communications with Pansy, he diligently scoured New York for a means of finding some.

"What you are looking for, Mr. Winter, cannot be found in New York." The speaker was a handsome, black-haired young man with full, sharply outlined lips—Winter hadn't quite gotten his name—at the office of the Philippines Mission to the United Nations. His neatly trimmed fingernail flicked the Xerox of Castle's handwritten copy of the violin message. "If your violin does come from the Muslim community in the Philippines, it comes from a time when some of them still wrote their languages in the Arabic script. They do not do that anymore. We are one country with a progressive national education system that teaches everyone to read the national language, Tagalog, and English as a second language. The Filipino Muslim people who come to the United States to study or to work are young. They study engineering and medicine to build their country. Some poor ones work here as taxi drivers or waiters in restaurants, but they would not be educated enough to help you.

"For what you want, you need a very old person, or a

scholar, or one of their religious leaders. Perhaps you should try in San Francisco. There is a greater interest in studying the Philippines there. Or in Saudi Arabia. Many Muslim Filipinos go to work in Saudi Arabia and other countries in the Persian Gulf."

Young Mr. Whoever's explanation and advice differed only slightly from what Castle had already heard a dozen times from other Filipino agencies and officials. As he left the office, with Mr. Whoever standing at the door smiling him out with a smile that looked like a tattoo, Castle thought of Pansy. Unfathomable, unattainable, unpredictable . . . her tumbling hair appeared before him as he had first seen it sitting behind her in the jury room. Her head turned. She fixed him with her limpid green eyes. Her purple lips spoke. *When you continually do the same sort of thing, Castle, and run into the same sort of dead end, you are failing to see the game as an adventure.*

Castle pondered and resolved to quit being ineffectual. He looked in the yellow pages for a Filipino restaurant. He found The Ferdinand. It was on East 37th Street. When he got to the address, he saw that the name had been changed to The Corazon. The portrait of President Aquino in a yellow dress above the cash register did not quite fill the rectangle of comparatively clean blue-green paint left by the portrait that had evidently preceded it. Apart from the president's portrait there was nothing in the decor to mar the restaurant's perfect International Formica style. Castle ordered Roast Pork Filipino from a cadaverous waiter with dry-looking brown skin.

"Pork not good to eat," replied the waiter under his breath. "Pigs dirty animals."

"I like roast pork," rejoined Castle indignantly. "Why's it on the menu if it isn't good?" He threw the last sentence at the skeletal waiter's departing back.

The waiter did not return. A squat, muscular, Hispanic-looking man who had been bussing dishes delivered the plate of roast pork to his table instead. It was not very good. Castle masticated a particularly challenging and resilient morsel and got an idea.

40

Why, he wondered, with a sense of Pansy somewhere in a dim recess of his brain urging him on, would a Filipino waiter make the busboy serve roast pork? Could it be that Moros consider it unclean to touch pork? A small but spirited voice piped from the recess in his brain: "You passed a man today who could have made you a million dollars if you had asked the right question."

"You wouldn't happen to be Muslim, would you?" asked Castle as the waiter refilled the water glass that Castle had drained to have an excuse to summon him.

"Yes. Muslim from Philippines," said the man dourly.

A sudden surge of adrenalin coursed through Castle's nervous system.

"This may sound a bit odd, but . . . You wouldn't happen to be able to tell me where I might find someone who can read some of the Moro language written in Arabic script . . . on the inside of a violin? Would you? Or wouldn't you?"

The waiter's papery skin pulled tighter against his cheek and jaw bones, until Castle thought it might tear. The man seemed to be experiencing an emotion, but Castle had no idea which one. He clenched his teeth and heard the blood surging noisily in his own temples.

"Mr. Osman will read violin. International Pacific Trade Corporation, Three-two-one West Twenty-fourth Street."

Castle shuddered as if he had received an electrical shock. "Thank you. I had just been wondering, you see." The waiter moved off in the direction of a pay phone in a far corner of the restaurant. Castle followed him with his eyes and forked a gobbet of pork fat covered with a congealing pink gravy into his mouth. Feigning nonchalance, he studied the picture of a daffodil on the tiny paper sugar pod that had been served with his tea. The waiter was making a telephone call.

Mr. Osman looked more Chinese than Filipino: matte-black hair combed back straight, full round face, epicanthically folded eyes wide open and lively behind large round glasses. He wore a white shirt, red necktie, and dark blue business suit made from a slightly shiny fabric. The Asian travel posters on the walls of his nondescript office bespoke the international side of his business. His conversation bespoke something else.

"You have the violin with you?" he asked with a nod and a smile.

Castle had not yet introduced himself; indeed, had not yet gotten beyond a tentative "Mr. Osman?" uttered from a standing position just inside the office door.

"You have the violin? please sit down." A single sentence of inscrutable syntax.

Castle sat down on the front edge of a leatherish chair. "My name is Castle Winter. You seem to have heard about my violin, or rather, *the* violin. It's not exactly mine, you see. I'm just interested in what's inside it. What I need is for someone to translate the lines in Arabic script written inside it. My . . . my informant suggested that you might do this for me?"

"You have the violin?" Mr. Osman smiled with the same cheerfulness he had evinced when the question first escaped his lips. Being closer to him now, Castle observed with interest that several of his upper teeth were set obliquely to their mates, but the effect was more a statement of humility—"I'm not one of those filthy rich Asian businessmen who can afford first-class dental work"—than a disfigurement. Castle's own painful dental history had made him a connoisseur of such effects.

"This is a Xerox of my handwritten copy of the inscription." Castle slid the paper onto Mr. Osman's desk. "I believe it is in some Moro language. I had gotten the impression you were a Muslim from the Philippines."

"No, I am from Hong Kong. Do you *have* the violin, Mr. Winter?"

"Can you read the message?"

"Not from this copy. Perhaps if I could look at the violin itself."

"It's a very careful copy. This mark here and here"—Castle pointed with a pencil to two semicircles with dots in them—"on top of the 'ains represent nasal sounds, I think. It's not an Arabic mark. I think it's derived from the Sanskrit *anasvara* mark which is also used to signify nasal sounds in Hindi. If so, that would point to Southeast Asia as the language area since Indian culture had a great impact there before Islam came to the region. Then, in addition, there's the number of consonants represented: seven fewer than in the basic Arabic alphabet. The *j*, *h*, and *kh* are missing, except here in line five in the name Muhammad, and then all four emphatics are missing, too. I judge this points to a language with a small number of consonants, like Indonesian or some related language."

Castle suddenly noticed that Mr. Osman was not attending to his discourse and withdrew his pencil.

"I understand you do not have the violin?" said Mr. Osman.

Castle sensed himself at a turning point. Having received Pansy's assurance that the violin was back in police hands, his answer to the question clearly should be no. On the other hand, Mr. Osman evidently knew about the violin, and his name was clearly Muslim (although Castle had never heard of a Chinese Muslim with a non-Chinese name). Hence, he was more than likely to know something about the inscription even if he couldn't translate it himself. Therefore, a yes answer might hold more promise of solving the mystery of the inscription than a no. Castle was not comfortable choosing untruth over honesty.

"Yes," he said after he had thoroughly ruminated on the moral dimensions of a lie and decided that it could not possibly have very serious consequences in this or any subsequent world. "I have the violin, but I thought it was easier just to bring the Xerox."

Mr. Osman scrutinized his face so intently that Castle was sure the word "liar" was written on it somewhere in itsybitsy print. Presently he looked down at the Xeroxed page.

"How much money do you think we will pay for the violin?"

"I recall hearing the figure of a hundred thousand dollars

mentioned," replied Castle, scarcely believing the words coming from his lips.

"The very sum the Mamadou woman wanted. Do you know Mamadou Mustafa, Mr. Winter?"

"A big black woman?"

"Yes. Bad temper."

"Only by reputation." Castle was beginning to enjoy talking like a movie detective. He wondered if he could work in a line like, "I want half the money now, Osman, and half when I deliver the goods."

"Miss Mamadou's violin, of course, was a crude fake."

"Had to be," growled Castle. "I've got the real one."

"Wonderful!" exclaimed Mr. Osman, sitting back in his chair and throwing out his arms expansively. "Then you can tell me the one thing that makes it different from an ordinary violin."

"It's on the paper in front of you, Osman." Castle stabbed the Xeroxed page with his forefinger.

"But the inscription is on the inside. It cannot be seen unless the violin is disassembled. So I cannot confirm that this is the correct writing. What is there, Mr. Winter, on the outside? A label, perhaps? A scratch?"

Castle thought.

Mr. Osman prompted him. "To discourage her from trying to cheat us further, I had the end part of Miss Mamadou's little finger cut off before she left the building."

Castle thought harder. Then he remembered.

"There are five grooves filed on the nut for strings going to the tuning pegs."

Mr. Osman sat forward and leaned across the desk. His smile now looked menacing, his uneven teeth those of a carnivorous animal. Castle was aware as he made the comparison in his mind that he was letting himself be unduly influenced by thoughts of fingers being cut off. And he didn't believe for an instant that anyone actually cut anyone else's finger off in the real world he was accustomed to living in. Nevertheless, Mr. Osman did look less friendly than before.

"We want the violin, Mr. Winter. I can pay you fifty thousand dollars now and an equal amount when you hand it over to us. If you don't hand it over, we will take it from you. Do you understand?"

Castle understood. "I don't have the violin," he stammered. "I was just kidding. Like in the movies. I just wanted to get someone to read . . ." He realized he was about to cry with fright.

"Then how do you know about the grooves on the nut?"

"I had the violin for a while. But I returned it to the police. Personally."

"You're lying. The police don't have it."

"They don't?" Castle was confused. "Are you sure they don't?"

"Absolutely certain."

"Well, I wonder why that is."

"So do I, Mr. Winter. Mamadou Mustafa told us her husband had acquired the violin, but then he died; and while she was negotiating with us over a reward, the violin fell into the hands of the police. Then when she went to pick it up, some young woman dressed like an Iranian revolutionary showed up to claim it also, and the police let her have it. When Miss Mamadou came here, she told me that after the Iranian woman sneaked out of the police station, she followed the boy who was with her to a computer store. She said she identified the woman working in the store, and she came up to her on the street and got her to give up the violin. But what she got was a substitute, with the top unglued and some scribbling in it. That was the violin she tried to sell to us.

"We subsequently checked with the police. They had a receipt the Iranian woman had signed, but apparently they had obtained no firm identification of her. They were quite apologetic and have promised to notify us if the violin comes back to them. So far, they have not notified us."

"But I did return it to the police after examining the inscription."

"So you say. Now, what I am asking myself, Mr. Winter, is who the young woman was who claimed the violin from the police. Miss Mamadou refused to divulge her name, obviously because she still expects to get the violin back and claim the reward. But you say you're only interested in the inscription inside it, so perhaps you might telephone her right now and have her bring the violin to the office. It is, after all, our property and not yours or hers."

This was not like the real world Castle had grown up in in the Midwest. There you might have a tense but friendly conversation with a neighbor for the purpose of getting the neighbor's son to return a bicycle he had swiped and been seen riding around on. No question about who owned the bike. No question of charging the boy with anything. But you wouldn't cut the boy's finger off if he returned the wrong bike. That just didn't sound right. Not nice; not real.

"I don't know about any young woman. A policeman I know saw the violin when people were talking about it in the property room at the police station. He knew I was interested in Arabic violin inscriptions, and he borrowed it to show it to me. I looked it over, made the copy I showed you, and returned it. I have no idea where the violin is now. I was astonished to hear of its value. I assure you, my sole interest is in getting the inscription translated. That's why I pretended at the beginning to have it. I wanted to excite your interest. But since you apparently can't help me, perhaps I should leave now and continue looking for someone who can."

Mr. Osman's smile never faltered. "I can see how uncomfortable it makes you to tell such a story, Mr. Winter. Your shoulders get stiff like this." He hunched his shoulders. "Your face gets white. I am afraid I have frightened you. I should never have mentioned . . . well, never mind. I have decided to send you to the one man who can translate your inscription. Will you follow me, please?"

Castle trailed the Chinese businessman out of his office and into a cavernous freight elevator that delivered them to a loft full of wooden crates and cardboard boxes in a variety of sizes. They stopped in front of a crate about six feet wide and six feet high.

"Mr. Winter, this is what I call a 'Marcos mummycase.'" He laughed. "I shipped many goods to and from the Philippines before Mr. Marcos was overthrown; I ship many goods now. I ship to many places. I have a very good business because I can deliver what people want. Before Mr. Marcos was overthrown, someone in the Philippines wanted me to stock some of these special crates in case of an urgent need. So now I still have them." Mr. Osman pulled on the front of the crate, which surprisingly swung out to reveal a small light-blue room within.

"There we are. First-class. You have a comfortable airline-style seat with a seat belt, a light, a chemical toilet on this side, a fan, a chest beside the seat here with some food and drinks, and these pockets on the inside of the door . . . I think a medicine kit, some reading material, and so forth. You could not be sent in finer style."

Castle felt paralyzed. He couldn't shift his eyes from a plastic plaque over the chemical toilet that said: IN CASE OF A WATER LANDING, UNDAMAGED CRATE WILL REMAIN AFLOAT.

"Sent? Sent where?"

"To Oman. To see our Master."

"I don't have a passport."

Mr. Osman laughed. "You won't need one."

Black unconsciousness saved Castle from feeling the pain of the sudden blow delivered to the back of his head by a Filipino workman who had materialized silently behind him with a heavy pipe in his hand.

7

Travelers departing New York City by way of John F. Kennedy Airport frequently experience moments of panic. Typically they occur on the way to the airport, and so they did for Castle Winter. He returned to consciousness belted into the airline seat in the tiny blue room. The light over his right shoulder was on. Jostling, bumping, and sensations of being lifted and put down alternated with periods of stillness. He wanted to scream and pound on the walls, but his terror at what might confront him if he escaped bound him tighter than the seatbelt. A trip to someplace, anyplace— had Mr. Osman said Oman?—was preferable to being killed, or even to having part of a finger cut off.

Becoming calmer, like a wild animal soothed by the very constriction of its cage, Castle reconsidered his preference for travel over death during what he took to be a transit from Manhattan through the Midtown Tunnel, followed by a series of head-on encounters with the car-eating mid-winter potholes of Queens. At the end of the ride, half-numb from vibration and jolting, he felt a forklift maneuver his crate about, carelessly banging it against other large objects. Then all was quiet. Castle pounded on the walls for a time and eventually slept.

Fresh jolts from another forklift woke him. Panic closed in again as he felt an elevator lift the crate into what he assumed was an airplane. Was the cargo compartment pressurized? Was the crate pressurized? Were either of them heated? He hysterically imagined himself arriving in freeze-dried condition and shattering into tiny flavor crystals on being unbelted from his seat.

Aloft at last and confident that the plane had climbed long enough for him to experience whatever dreadful effects altitude might bring, Castle relaxed. The reading matter was all in Chinese except for an Arabic Koran, placed there, according to the gold lettering on its plastic cover, by the Pahlavani Publishing Committee. The food container was stocked with canned soft drinks and packages of snacks that Castle guessed came from vending machines in Mr. Osman's building. The freshness date stamped on a package of cupcakes had not expired, but Castle suspected that the period of so-called freshness after baking of that particular product was measured in years.

Castle slept. He dreamed of Judith. They were playing tennis. She was tawny and athletic and played aggressively. A white ribbon held her straw-colored hair in a bouncy ponytail. She won. He awoke. He daydreamed of Pansy. He realized with disappointment that he was so captivated by her cranial bumps, her auburn mane, and her green-eyed, black-lipped face that he could not call to mind those more seductive details of bodily proportion and curvature upon which truly lurid daydreams are built.

After twelve hours he stopped doing and thinking anything. He simply endured, half asleep, dully sensitive to the occasional changes in the whirrs, bumps, and vibrations that enveloped his room. The realization came to him that a long air trip in a packing crate in cargo differed very little from a long air trip in the passenger cabin. Once he turned the light off, but the absolute darkness was terrifying, and he immediately turned it on again.

Exactly a day after being hit on the head in Mr. Osman's loft, and two hours after landing, being unloaded, traveling somewhere in a truck, and being unloaded again, Castle heard an unlocking sound and saw the doorhandle of his little blue chamber move slowly down and then back up. There was no further sound. He waited five minutes and tried the door himself. It opened.

He was alone in a first-class hotel room.

A basket of choice fruit in a clear plastic wrapping reposed on the low bureau. The card read:

Compliments of the Manager
Royal Musqat Mayflower Hotel

Musqat was the capital city of Oman. Castle looked out the window. He saw a white beach and a blue sea under a cloudless sky. Craning his neck to look directly down he saw the side of a swimming pool surrounded by aluminum and plastic lounge chairs on an artificial grass carpet. He turned from the window and searched the room for confirmation of his whereabouts. Every item of furniture would have looked equally appropriate in a hotel room in Kansas City.

However, the table beside the bed yielded a Koran, placed there by the Pahlavani Publishing Committee, and screwed to the plastic top of the built-in bureau was a green plastic disk bearing an arrow in white outline and the word "Mecca" in Arabic. The laundry bags and slips in the closet were printed in Arabic and English, as was the room service menu. A small prayer rug was folded on a closet shelf.

Castle looked in the mirror. His checked suit and white shirt were rumpled from the trip and his lush wavy black hair disarranged, but otherwise he looked quite normal: a bit haggard, perhaps, but the familiar square chin, full mouth, sculpted cheekbones, and dark, romantic eyes. Unshaven, of course, but only to a degree that was considered stylish by professional baseball players and young actors portraying cops on television. His right eyebrow jumped. He touched the still tender lump on the back of his head.

A banana from the fruit basket tasted delicious. As he ate it he thought. What would Judith have him do? Telephone the American Embassy. What would Pansy have him do? Explore. He rose and went to the door. It was unlocked.

The corridor outside was empty. It looked like the one in a motel he had recently stayed in near Poughkeepsie, except here the rooms were numbered with Arabic-Arabic numerals instead of European-Arabic numerals. He closed the door, picked up the telephone, and dialed zero.

"Reception. May I help you?" The voice sounded Indian.

"Is this the hotel reception desk?" He felt deeply confused.

"Yes."

"I'm Mr. Winter in room . . . I'm afraid I don't know what room I'm in."

"Six-oh-three, Mr. Winter."

"Thank you."

"Will there be anything else, sir?"

"Yes. Could you tell me what country I'm in?"

"The Sultanate of Oman, sir."

"You're quite certain."

"Yes, sir. Will there be anything else, sir?"

"Yes, would you please connect me with the consular section of the American Embassy in Musqat."

"Yes, sir. Please stay on the line."

After assorted clicks and buzzes a new voice came on the line.

"United States Embassy, Mr. Kimbrough speaking."

"Is this the American Embassy in Musqat, Oman?"

"Yes, sir. May I help you?"

"I hope so." Castle was feeling much relieved. "My name is Castle Winter."

"Oh, hello, Mr. Winter. Are you feeling better?"

Castle withdrew the telephone an inch from his ear to think. "Better?" he said cautiously. "I'm feeling quite well, thank you, considering that I was knocked on the head, kidnapped, and brought to Oman against my will in a locked crate in a cargo plane."

"Of course," replied Kimbrough placatingly. "Dr. Fernandez has told us about your unfortunate situation, and we're doing everything we can to help."

"Who's Dr. Fernandez?"

"Do you remember? After you called the first time? A doctor visited you and examined you? Dr. Fernandez? Thin, dark, Filipino gentleman?"

Castle felt his chest tighten. "No, I don't remember. No doctor has seen me, and I haven't called you before. Your name is Kimberly?"

"Kimbrough."

"I'd like to speak to the Ambassador, Mr. Kimbrough."

"Unfortunately, the Ambassador isn't available, Mr. Winter. But I think we in the consular section can do everything we need to do to help you. Dr. Fernandez brought us your passport. Do you remember the name of your doctor in New York?"

"I don't have a passport with me."

"That's no problem. We have it right here. We'll return it to you shortly. We sent the passport over to Mr. Dentisto to have the visa checked. Everything is in order. Your company has properly arranged for your visit. We received the passport back from him just before you called, and we'll have it delivered to the hotel tomorrow. Room six-oh-three?"

"Yes. Who's Mr. Dentisto?"

"Mr. Antonio Dentisto is an Englishman who works for the Sultan keeping track of all visas issued to Europeans and Americans. Unofficially, I can tell you that no one gets into Oman from the West without his say-so. If he says that it's okay for you to be here, it's okay. You don't have anything to worry about. No one's going to kick you out of the country."

"But I want to be kicked out of the country! I don't have any clothes! I've been kidnapped!"

"If you'll just hold on, Mr. Winter, I'll have someone see if Dr. Fernandez is free to stop by the hotel when he gets off at the hospital."

"I don't want to see Dr. Fernandez! I don't want to see any Filipinos! Don't you see? They're the ones who've set this up! Fernandez must work for Osman!"

"I'll tell you what, Mr. Winter," said Kimbrough soothingly. "Go down to the lobby and take a taxi to the embassy. I can stay here until six o'clock, which should give you plenty of time. I don't think it's wise for you to be staying in the hotel alone."

"Thank you, Mr. Kimbrough. I'm very grateful. How do I get to the embassy?"

"Tell the driver *'as-safarat al-amrikiya.'* Can you say that?"

"Yes. I read and speak some Arabic."

"Well, good for you, Mr. Winter! Most American businessmen who come out here don't know a word."

"But I'm not a businessman."

"I'll see you in a little bit, Mr. Winter. Good-bye."

Castle looked at himself in the mirror. He straightened his coat and tie. The normal-looking, fortyish man he was looking at certainly didn't look like the sort of person who would get a visa, travel to Oman, check into a hotel, then forget that it had all happened and hallucinate a bizarre alternative explanation for being there. Kimbrough would surely see that.

All of the men at Reception looked Indian or Pakistani. The one who looked up as Castle approached had a deep brown jowly face with a heavy black mustache, but he was dressed in a dark blue business suit and white shirt. A white name placard on his breast pocket said MR. AHMAD in Roman letters. Glancing around, Castle noticed that the only person in Arab garb in the luxurious, almost deserted lobby was squatting behind a polished bronze brazier tending several Arab coffeepots nestled in the coals.

"Hello, my name's Castle Winter. I'm an American."

"Of course, Mr. Winter. I was on duty when you checked in yesterday. I hope you are feeling better. The doctor said that you needed much sleep so we did not disturb you."

Castle held steady in his course. "I would like a taxi to go to the American Embassy."

"Very good, sir. What time in the morning would you like it to come for you?"

"I don't want it in the morning. I want it now."

"Very good, sir. I will see what I can do."

Mr. Ahmad spoke on the telephone in a language that was

certainly not Arabic. Castle noted by the cashier's desk a framed sign giving the conversion rates from various currencies into Omani riyals.

"I'm very sorry, Mr. Winter. You see, it is now almost five o'clock, and there will be no taxis until tomorrow morning."

"But I see four taxis parked outside right now," said Castle with a raised voice.

"Those have been sent by various ministries and companies for other guests. We are so far from Musqat and Matrah—twenty miles, you see—that taxis must be ordered. But the taxi offices do not take calls after five o'clock."

"But that's ridiculous! What if someone wants to go to a play or a concert?"

"Well, you see, we don't have plays and concerts in Oman."

"But what do tourists do who want to get around?"

"We have very few tourists in Oman. People come to Oman on business. Or they are invited by a ministry."

"Don't they go to restaurants at night?"

Mr. Ahmad smiled broadly. "When they do, Mr. Winter, they come here. On the lower level. Very nice restaurants with European and American food. I shall order a taxi for you for eight in the morning. I suggest that you go to the restaurant, Mr. Winter, and then have a good night's sleep. Traveling is very exhausting."

Castle started to wander away from the reception desk. Then he turned and said sharply, "How can you order a taxi for eight in the morning if the offices are closed?"

Mr. Ahmad flashed a very white, toothy smile. "I shall tell the night receptionist, and he will telephone at seven when the offices open again."

Castle swayed on his feet and caught himself on the polished railing that surrounded the sunken center of the lobby. He felt suddenly like a week-old party balloon, a soft and puckered membrane losing its buoyancy and ready to make its final descent to the floor and oblivion. He willed himself alert. I'm not sick or crazy, he thought. I'm hungry and tired.

Spaghetti bolognese and chef's salad with house dressing were served by a sallow young man in black trousers and a red waistcoat. Castle elicited the information that he was from Sri Lanka, did not know Dr. Fernandez, and would happily charge the meal to room 603.

Until halfway through a piece of stale chocolate cake he regretted ordering, Castle was the only diner. Then a blond man in sunglasses and a garish yellow Hawaiian shirt came in and loudly ordered a steak in a distinctively American accent. Castle imagined Pansy giving him one of her appraising looks. This is the man who will give me a million dollars if I ask him the right question, he thought.

As it turned out, he wasn't. His name was Fred. United States Air Force. Regular supply flight from Europe to the navy base at Diego Garcia. Always stopped over in Oman, but prohibited by military rules from leaving the hotel. "Way it is, Castle, we keep this here low profile in Oman, see. This the Brits' territory. Brits run the army, run the gummint, tell the Sultan what to eat for breakfast. Sultan got himself educated in England, see, and the Brits helped him kick his pa off the throne. So Brits say they want keep Oman for themselves, American Air Force keep outta sight. But stick around, Castle. Round eleven or so, the stewardesses might show up. British Airways. The nightclub opens up." Castle followed Fred's pointing finger and saw a low arched doorway in the stucco wall with NIGHTCLUB written above it in unlit neon tubing. "Truth is," continued Fred, "it's usually boring as hell. But you never know, do you."

Castle decided not to tell Fred about being shipped to Oman in a packing crate. But he went to bed strangely satisfied at having talked to a normal person.

An eight o'clock call informing Castle that his car was waiting found him dressed and eating his second succulent orange. At Reception a man with a black beard trimmed to a narrow line along his jaw and coming to a point at his chin offered to take him to his car. He was wearing sandals, a tightly wound black turban, and a white gown cinched at the waist by a gold studded belt, into which was thrust a large dagger in a tooled silver sheath that turned sharply to the right below the belt. Castle followed him to a maroon Mercedes parked under the hotel's canopy.

"*As-safarat al-amrikiya*," said Castle as he settled himself in the back seat. The driver did not respond. The man in the black turban got into the passenger's seat in front. "*Uridu an adhhaba ila as-safarat al-amrikiya.*"

"Your Arabic is very good," replied the man in the turban in a cultured English accent.

Since awakening Castle had had the euphoric feeling that what had happened the day before had not really happened at all. After all, hadn't the crate disappeared from his room during dinner? Now the euphoria suddenly evaporated. "I want to go to the American Embassy," he said anxiously. "I have an appointment with Mr. Kimbrough. He's expecting me. This morning. Very soon."

Castle sat back. He realized that he had no way at all of telling whether or not they were headed for the embassy. Probably customary to send a translator with the driver if the customer is European, he thought. Couldn't be too many Omani taxi drivers who spoke English. He was amused at how readily he had let himself slip back into yesterday's paranoia.

They were cruising down a spacious divided highway that looked as if it had been finished the week before. Piles of sand and construction debris were scattered along the sides between widely separated driveways leading to large, grand-looking buildings. Most of the buildings were still under construction. Clusters of workers milled around more piles of sand and construction debris.

Castle fleetingly glimpsed Arabic words on passing signs: Ministry of Something, Department of Something Else, Whatever Research Institute . . . he could only catch a word or two before they had passed. A green sign directed traffic for Matrah to take a left fork. Castle had read on the back of the menu in the restaurant that Matrah was the port city adjacent to Musqat, the capital. Another green sign directed traffic for Musqat to keep to the two left lanes and Nizwa traffic to take the right lane. The Mercedes took the right lane.

Castle lurched forward. *"As-safarat al-amrikiya. Bi Musqat. Musqat. Sayyid* Kimbrough . . . *Kimburo* . . . *Kimburu."*

The black turban turned and the bearded face smiled back at Castle. "First we'll go to Nizwa, and then to Mr. Kimbrough. Nizwa is one of the most interesting towns in Oman. It's at the foot of the Green Mountains, the center of the date industry. It will take us about two hours. On the way, I can tell you about Oman. Whatever you would like to know."

"Who are you?"

"Khalid. I escort visitors."

"Who sent you to escort me?"

"I work for a section of the Ministry."

"What ministry?"

"It is a section headed by Mr. Dentisto. We receive visitors to Oman."

"Do you know that I was kidnapped and brought to Oman in a packing crate? With an airline seat in it? Painted blue inside? And someone named Dr. Fernandez told the American Embassy that I was crazy? I didn't have a passport, but the Embassy says it has my passport. I didn't have a visa, but the Embassy says Mr. Dentisto said my visa is valid. Do you know about all this, Khalid?" Castle looked at the back of Khalid's turban and then at the back of the driver's embroidered pillbox-shaped skullcap. "I'm not making it up."

Khalid did not turn his head, which made his reply sound eerily disembodied. "Everything will become clear at Nizwa, Mr. Winter."

Pansy left Software City and turned left toward the 59th Street IRT station. She didn't notice the heavy black woman in denim overalls and blue peajacket matching steps beside her until she spoke.

"You still got my violin, honey. You forget that? You think

you can hand Mamadou a piece of shit and say it's a banana? Not on your little white ass you can't. We gonna talk, and you gonna tell Mamadou where that violin's at."

Like any properly acclimated New Yorker, Pansy stared straight ahead and kept walking. She didn't even glance at Mamadou, but when she looked the other direction at the corner of 62nd to check whether a stretch limo was actually going to run the red light or was just bluffing, she caught a glimpse of two young black men walking in step together a few feet behind her.

"We talkin' serious shit here, honey. Me and the brothers gonna stick by you, see you can't remember where that violin at."

The intimidating trio stood near her on the crowded downtown platform. Pansy stared at the floor thinking furiously. She counted the number of black chewing gum stains on a three-foot-square section of concrete. Then she looked around and counted the squares from one side of the platform to the other and from one of the I-beam roof support pillars to the next. She multiplied the product by the number of pillars from the downtown to the uptown end of the platform.

"There are 32,400 chewing gum stains on this platform," she said in a loud, animated voice. A man in a trench coat festooned with useless straps and buttons looked at her sideways. "Thirty stops brings you to just short of a million wads of gum spit out."

The man looked around to see if anyone was observing a deranged female punk, probably on crack, accosting him. A fat black woman and two athletic-looking black men, one with a three-inch-high flat-top, were looking straight at the two of them. Everyone else was pretending nothing was happening.

"Throw in the West Side. 'Course you have to multiply it all by two because of the platform on the uptown side. Right there you're talking, let's say, four million. And that's just the IRT. BMT and IND probably double that total, which makes eight million for Manhattan. The other boroughs are less crowded; maybe all of them together don't add up to as much as Manhattan. So I'd say fifteen million gobs of gum rubbed into all the subway floors right this very minute." Pansy cocked her head at her nonplussed target. "You ever do estimating? I read a book on it. It changed my entire life. For example, how long do you think a gum stain lasts before people wear it away with their shoes? Come on, how long?"

The man cleared his throat awkwardly. "Maybe two months? How should I know?"

"Don't give up on yourself. You've got to have confidence. Two months sounds good. Maybe four months in the boroughs because they have less traffic. So that means that every four months you've got sixteen million pieces of gum spit out in Manhattan and seven million more in the boroughs for a total of, what, twenty-three million spits. That's estimating."

"Yes, I suppose it is," replied the man.

"You don't get it, though, do you. The mystery is: Who's doing all that spitting? How often have you actually seen someone spit a piece of gum on a platform? Right. Maybe never. And then you never seen any of it fresh. It's always black and worn in like it's been there a while. It makes you wonder." Pansy cocked her head fetchingly to the other side.

"Wonder what?"

"Whether the transit police and the maintenance people come in in the middle of the night and spit gum. Just to make it seem more like New York."

The man grinned. "A huge conspiracy."

"Something like that. By the way, you got any gum?"

"No."

"I do." She pulled a pack of sugarless gum out of her pocket and offered him a stick with a big smile. He took it and unwrapped it. "And speaking of conspiracy," she continued in a softer voice, "if you don't let me tag along with you for a while, those three people staring at us are going to follow me home and beat me up."

"What?" The man looked over to find that Mamadou and her companions had suddenly turned away.

"I'll tell you all about it. Do you play text adventures?"

8

Castle tried to control his rapidly beating heart. If all would be explained at Nizwa, he could surely wait until they got to Nizwa. As they progressed from the coastal plain into the gray stony hills, the more prominent of which were topped by small round stone forts or lookout towers, Castle tried to divert himself by looking at his surroundings. Was he not, after all, in Oman, one of the most obscure and difficult to visit countries in the world?

They skirted the foot of a mountain range, passing few villages. Aside from occasional camels and goats grazing on a scattering of dry-looking bushes, there seemed to be little life among the stones.

They stopped at a large and prosperous-looking village with mud-walled date gardens and a huge abandoned castle or caravan depot. Khalid was ignorant of the age or history of the half-ruined structure, but it was, he said, the usual sight to stop and see on the road to Nizwa. A narrow stream of water gurgled from an underground tunnel dug into the aquifer of the mountainside behind the village and flowed beside the walls and then into the date gardens. The saplings and grass along its banks lent a bright green accent to the stony landscape. Three young children were swimming naked in a deep pool where the stream passed under a footbridge. With the ragged facade of the ruined caravansary rising behind the children, Castle thought it one of the most idyllic scenes he had ever witnessed. He wondered if he would ever in his whole life have gotten to Oman except by packing crate.

Trailing Khalid back toward the highway, Castle found that the driver had driven the Mercedes into the stream where it rippled over a wide bed of pebbles. He was washing the car with his white gown tucked up around his waist. Beneath the gown he wore an Indian-style men's skirt in an orange and yellow floral print. Castle wondered if Khalid, who was the picture of severe elegance in his black turban, silver dagger, and spotless white gown tied at the top with dangling gold tassels, was wearing an equally garish and un-Arab undergarment.

The countryside became noticeably greener as they penetrated the jagged mountains, but a rocky gray remained the predominant color. Nizwa's extensive date groves preceded the town, which turned out to be a large assemblage of flat-roofed, two- and three-story mud brick buildings completely surrounded by the palms. The domed mosque in the town's center looked new, but behind and above it loomed a vast and imposing structure of obviously greater antiquity. This was an enormous round fortress built of brick and stone with a crenellated parapet and rifle or cannon ports two-thirds of the way up its otherwise featureless walls. Castle guessed that the fortress was at least fifty feet tall and probably two hundred feet in diameter.

The Mercedes stopped at a plain arched entrance fitted with heavy wooden doors beneath a fluorescent light fixture.

"This is the fortress of Nizwa," said Khalid helpfully. "It is very interesting to visit."

Castle got out into the bright sun and followed Khalid through the doorway. A group of guards was lounging in the shade of a vaulted tunnel behind the entranceway. At the sight of Castle they lined up and stood at a kind of attention with their old bolt-action rifles at order arms. Castle looked at them. Four were dressed in white, the fifth in faded bluish green. The mismatched guard had a grizzled spade-shaped beard about six inches long and a turban of purple and white striped material that looked about right for a beach towel. The edge of a bright orange underskirt showed below the hem of his gown. The white-gowned guards were also bearded, the youngest sporting a goatee like Khalid's, another a long straggly fringe of black and gray with no mustache, the third equally long but less straggly white whiskers, and the last a short, neat white beard that would have made him look more soldierly than the rest if he hadn't seemed to be using his rifle as a crutch to lean on. Their minimum age appeared to be around sixty.

"You may give them money if you wish to," said Khalid diffidently. Castle knew he had three subway tokens and three pennies in his pocket because he had counted them several times when reviewing his resources back at the hotel. "They are veterans appointed by the Sultan," said Khalid. "You may also take their picture."

"Could you apologize for me, Khalid," said Castle. "I don't have money or a camera."

"There's no need to apologize," replied Khalid. "They are simply accustomed to things from visitors. We will go inside."

The way inside led through two stone tunnels and then up a steep, narrow staircase. At last they emerged again into the sunshine of a large circular area about twenty feet below the parapet. Several covered doorways like the one they had exited from rose above the floor level indicating the location of other stairways. Small windows only a few inches above the stone pavement penetrated the wall in a dozen places. At some of them antique cannons on newly restored wooden cradles pointed over the endless date gardens. A stone stairway led up to the crumbling parapet, where riflemen had once aimed at their enemies through slits in the stone. Castle wondered if the veterans below had ever fought in the fort, and if so, against whom.

"What's this?" asked Castle, pointing into a deep shaft some four feet square at his feet.

"Punishment," said Khalid. "Men were put in there. Forgotten."

"This place is incredible. It's like something out of *Ivanhoe*."

"*Ivanhoe* has always seemed to me like something out of Oman," said Khalid.

"How long has the fort been open for visitors?"

"About ten years. Before that there was war with the people in the mountains. It's been closed for repairs now for three months."

Castle was staring out of a cannon port. "How do you mean, closed for repairs?"

Khalid did not reply. Castle turned around. Khalid was nowhere to be seen. But Castle was not alone. A dozen armed men in white gowns and turbans had silently materialized from the several stairway doors. They were standing in a group around the old spade-bearded guard in the blue-green gown and purple-striped turban.

"Where is Khalid? *Wain Khalid?* Khalid is my guide. *Khalid murshidi*." Some of the armed men laughed and again fell silent. "What's funny?" said Castle, his heart rising in his throat. "*Ana amrikani*. I don't have money or a camera." He tried to remember how to say "I don't have" in Arabic.

The old guard and a younger, white-gowned man wearing crossed bandoliers loaded with cartridges stepped forward. The old man looked deeply into Castle's face.

"I'm sorry, I just don't have any money," said Castle desperately. "I was kidnapped. I came in a packing crate. Subway tokens, that's all."

The old man extracted a rolled piece of paper from behind the gold-chased dagger sheath thrust through his belt. He extended it toward Castle. Castle took it and unrolled it. It was the Xeroxed copy of the violin message he had given to Mr. Osman in New York.

"Shaikh Zakariya wants to know about the violin," said the younger man in British-accented English.

"Of course," said Castle, in a voice bordering on hysteria, "that's why I'm here. To tell you about the violin, and you to tell me what the writing means. But if you don't want to tell me what the writing means, that's perfectly okay. I understand it's probably a secret of some kind that people like me shouldn't know about. But that's okay." He looked at the stern faces fixed on him. "The violin. Well, as I said to Mr. Osman—Mr. Osman? Your friend in New York?—anyway, I told Mr. Osman that I was serving on a special narcotics grand jury. I know you're going to want to know what a special narcotics grand jury is, and I'm not sure I can really explain it since it doesn't really do anything in particular except agree with the district attorney. Later. So, I was on this jury, and the violin was entered in evidence. But it had actually been stolen from somebody. But my friend got it from the police so I could look at it because I used to study Arabic. This isn't making much sense, is it?"

"Do you have the violin?"

"No. I gave it to my friend to return to the police."

"Did your friend return it to the police?"

"She says she did, but Mr. Osman says she didn't. I don't know. She's a little flaky. Crazy?"

"Do you know where is the violin?"

"No, I do not."

"Do you know Moosa Makki?"

"Moosa Makki? No, I don't believe I do."

"If he thinks you have the violin, he will kill you to get it. Do you know what the violin means?"

"No, I do not. And I am no longer sure I want to."

"The violin you had was the right one. The writing is correct. Did you play it?"

"It had no strings."

"That is safer. But you had it. Your life will change. The violin changes people's lives."

The old guard stepped closer and looked into Castle's face from six inches away. Castle tried to place his odor and suddenly realized that his beard was scented with rosewater.

"*Sahih*," said the old man, backing away again.

"He says you are speaking the truth. He will continue to look for the violin."

The armed men casually turned and headed back toward the covered doorways. It was as if a drama had ended, and the audience was drifting away chatting about what they had seen. Castle remained paralyzed. He could think of nothing to say. Most of the men had disappeared down the stairways when he finally called out, "Is my car waiting for me down below?"

The old man in the bluish-green gown and the younger man who had done the speaking turned and leveled their rifles. Their two shots rang as one, and Castle slumped to the stone pavement unable to move his legs. Pain shot throughout his body from the backs of his thighs. He felt strong hands gripping his shoulders and dragging him across the stones. The pain intensified. All he could see was the color red. Then he felt suspended in space, being lowered. The hands let go. He dropped. The pain when he hit the bottom surpassed bearing, and he felt no more.

Frankie walked into a music store on 47th Street just off Times Square. A gargantuan black-bearded man wearing a yarmulke looked down at him from behind the glass counter with a mixture of contempt and indifference. Frankie swaggered as he approached the giant.

"Yo, you got violin strings?"

The proprietor pulled open a drawer and pulled out four plastic bags which he plopped one by one on the counter.

"And I need one of those wood things that stands up in the middle for the strings."

The proprietor extracted a bridge from a second drawer.

"And a bow."

This required a trip to the back room, but the proprietor returned presently with a violin bow. Frankie took it and nodded appraisingly as he hefted it and swung it like a baton.

"You want to know, maybe, how to get to Carnegie Hall?" said the proprietor as he deposited Frankie's money in the cash register and tore off the receipt. Frankie picked up his paper bag and headed out the door. "Practice!" roared the fat man with a loud guffaw.

"Asshole," said Frankie under his breath.

9

Dark and cold. Castle heard the scrabbling of someone climbing down into the pit. Strong hands pulled him to a sitting position, causing searing pain to spark from the backs of his thighs to every part of his body. The hands passed a rope under his arms. Again the scrabbling sounds. Then the rope bit painfully into his armpits and made him gasp for breath as he was drawn jerkily upward. His wounded legs scraped heavily over the stone lip of the pit, and he relapsed into unconsciousness in a red flash of pain.

Hot and bright. Sunlight glittered around the edges of a white cloth stretched across the small window to Castle's right. He had woken to pain and sweat and was groggily surveying his surroundings from a prone position on a narrow iron cot. His thighs ached and throbbed. Squatting in the corner was a brown-skinned teenage boy dressed in a white gown and skullcap. When he saw Castle looking at him, he grinned.

"Good morning, sir. What a beautiful hunk of man-flesh you are today."

Castle had read about people confusing dreams with reality and wondered.

From his other side a refined, almost affected, but distinctively American voice said, "Good afternoon. How are you feeling?" Castle turned his head and saw a deeply lined, ravished-looking face gazing down at him. The man's build and posture seemed young, making his deep jowl lines, crinkly eyes, and furrowed forehead look more a product of wear than of age. He seemed vaguely familiar. "Don't mind Abdallah. That's the only English I've taught him. He says it every morning when he brings my tea. Sets me up for the whole day. How are you feeling?"

"I hurt. My legs," said Castle, aware he was slurring his words.

"A very good Filipino doctor gave you a shot to make you sleep, and you're supposed to take a pill to put you back to sleep after you've had some nice tea." At the word "tea," Abdallah slipped quietly from the room. "The doctor took the bullets out and says there's nothing to worry about. No real harm done. Shaykh Zack isn't the kind of person to hurt someone permanently."

"Shaykh Zack. Who's he? Who are you? I think I've met you."

"John Anderson." Castle grasped a proffered hand and found it as lifeless as his own. "Ah, here's tea."

Abdallah placed a bronze tray laden with pot and cups on a wooden table next to Castle's cot. He poured for two. John Anderson held out a cup to Castle, at the same time extending toward him a pink capsule tweezered between his thumb and ring finger.

"Pilly first, then the tea. Doctor insists."

"The only Filipino doctor I know of is a criminal," said Castle weakly after washing the capsule down with the strong sweet tea.

"Oh my," replied John Anderson flatly. "My mistake. What a *faux pas*. I suppose I should have called somebody else. Do you belong to an HMO, perhaps? I guess that's not fair. After all, you are wounded. You rest now. We can have a chat when you wake up."

Castle shut his eyes, undecided whether to encourage the dream to continue. When he opened them again, Abdallah and Anderson were gone. Instead, the castle guard with the long straggly black and white beard squatted ominously by the door staring fixedly at him from under his voluminous turban. His antique bolt-action rifle was balanced across his knees, and the bent tip of a sheathed dagger protruded from the belt of cartridges around his waist. Castle stared apprehensively at the fearsome, weathered face. The guard gazed back unblinking. After a minute he spoke.

"So you don't recognize me. Good. I hoped you wouldn't."

"Anderson?"

The guard stood up and peeled off his beard and large pock-marked nose. Then he untied the loose folds of his faded mustard turban. The fringe of graying blond hair with a few long strands pulled across his balding pate instantly made him look American again.

"I was so upset when you said you thought you recognized me. They say that when Lawrence of Arabia disguised himself as an Arab in Cairo, the Arabs would see him lurking around and say, 'Look, there goes that silly Brit again.' I just couldn't bear it if they said that about me. That's why I never put this on when Abdallah's around. My little secret."

"Who?" said Castle like a fledgling owl.

"Abdallah's my boy. Oh, you mean, 'Who am I?' Well, my dear, who haven't I been? Who I am now is the United States Drug Enforcement Administration's undercover agent in Nizwa secretly monitoring the production and distribution of Green Mountain Blue. A-a-and—segue on a dramatic rising note—the Sultan of Oman's undercover agent posing on occasion as an ancient retainer appointed to the castle guard but actually assigned to keep track of what the United States Drug Enforcement Administration is doing in the interior of his country. A-a-and—grand finale—the undercover agent of some British agency, although I'm not exactly sure which one, assigned to collect intelligence on any unreported contacts between the Sultan's government and the DEA. Pretty good for a Harvard graduate, isn't it? Most of us are forced by wretched circumstance into banking or stock brokerage."

Castle closed his eyes to deny everything around him. "How can I get home? I just want to go home."

"In good time, intrepid adventurer. We were talking about me, do you remember? It's rude to interrupt. Well, I started out, you see, as a Peace Corps volunteer in Afghanistan. My dear, I don't want to tell you how many years ago that was. I parted company with those wonderful people after four months. It's not an interesting story or one that casts much credit upon the Peace Corps' tolerance of diversity.

"By that time I'd fallen absolutely in love with the costumes. In Cambridge I used to spend two hours in the morning picking out my clothes and getting dressed, and no one ever came up to me and said, 'John, what a wonderful combination!' The reason, of course, was my face. It's ruined, isn't it? Everyone can see it. Has been since I was twenty. Directly from adolescent pimples to old age. I simply don't know how it happened. Genes, I expect. What I wouldn't give for your Adonis looks! A face made for kissing. But my body, my body, now, which I gather from the look on your face fails to interest you, is superb. I was an incredibly good dancer once. I bet you weigh close to two hundred pounds, but I pulled you out of that nasty pit and carried you out of the fort all by myself.

"Well anyhow, let's face it. In Afghanistan how you dress is who you are. They don't have the American obsession with pretty faces. And the variety of costumes? My dear, you wouldn't believe. My wardrobe will positively amaze you. I can dress up as anything. So after I left Afghanistan, I stayed for a few years in Pakistan doing a little dealing and a little smuggling. Learning a few languages. Just what everyone else was doing, of course, though I'm rather better at the languages than most.

"But then that nasty war became big business, and I didn't feel as welcome. Can you believe those Saudis standing by the road at the Afghan border with bags of money and handing out packs of it like chocolate bars to *mujahideen* going across? I'm telling you."

"How can I get home?" said Castle with tears in his voice.

Anderson sighed in resignation. "You can lead a horse to

water. All right. You are scheduled on a flight from Musqat to New York by way of Cairo and Frankfurt two weeks from today. The doctor said you should be able to sit by then if he shoots you full of painkiller."

Castle tried to think through his discomfort and grogginess. "Passport," he said at length. "I don't have a passport. How can I get into the U.S.?"

"Really, Mr. Winter. You are in the hands of the DEA. We're a law unto ourselves. We can do anything. And even if we can't, you'll be carrying that very super forgery the Pahlavanis gave the embassy in Musqat to make sure they would ignore any call for help you might make. They think of everything, the Pahlavanis. Extraordinary people, really."

"Who are the Pahlavanis?"

"My dear," said Anderson caustically, "if you had let me continue with my story, you would have found out by now. But you weren't interested so I'm not sure I shall tell you. Yes, I shall. While we're eating. Abdallah will be back in half an hour to start dinner. I'll leave you alone and put my clothes away."

Dinner was rice and a vegetable stew flavored with curry. Between mouthfuls Anderson extolled the virtues of a vegetarian regime. Castle ate slowly, testing his appetite. Anderson finished and nibbled on a fresh date.

"It's unbelievable how they can take these wonderful fruits from the Garden of Eden, run them through the Nizwa factory, and transform them into a compressed black brick of cloying sweetness and revolting appearance. But I promised you more of my story. You should feel honored. Nobody ever gets to hear my story.

"So there I was in Rawalpindi, in Pakistan, building up this wonderful collection of clothes"—Anderson had exchanged his white gown for a maroon Pakistani-style tunic and pantaloons covered with garish green embroidery—"when I met Boulos, this homesick Egyptian working in the U.N.'s economic development office there. I was able to get him some Johnny Walker, which he desperately needed to treat his homesickness, and he in the course of things became expansive and told me about what he called 'the famous colored cotton plants of Oman.'

"The story went that the Omanis once wanted some agricultural development aid. But there wasn't anything to develop except dates, and the date factory was already contracted. So they invented a story about a kind of cotton that had naturally colored fibers. Red, blue, and so forth. They said it grew in parts of the Green Mountains that had unique soil and climate conditions. For a few hundred thousand dollars, production could be expanded and modernized, and Oman could export at an advantage because textile mills could save dyeing costs. I asked Boulos what happened, and he said the Omanis got their money without ever having to show anyone the plants. And of course there were never any plants to show. It was just a fiddle to get the money."

Anderson laughed at the recollection. "I thought it was wonderful! So I got thinking about it, and I experimented with dyeing dope. *What . . . a . . . mess*! But I finally got a block of hashish, mixed with some other things, you know, to soup it up, that had a very nice dark blue tint to it. Not too garish. Nothing phony looking. Voilà! Green Mountain Blue! I sold a few blocks and then took some to the DEA people in Islamabad, which is where the government people live next door to Rawalpindi. I knew them because I had sold smuggled X-rated videotapes to them.

"One thing led to another, and they hired me to work undercover within what they termed 'the international drug culture' to trace the source of Green Mountain Blue and keep tabs on it. Fortunately, some of my Peace Corps friends had sufficient loyalty to give me glowing letters of recommendation.

"After that I had to choose between the Green Mountains in Oman and the Green Mountains in Libya, but Oman was more exotic. The DEA set it all up for me to come. My 'cover' is that I visit periodically to advise the Nizwa date factory on management."

Castle ate one brownish orange date after another. He couldn't remember ever having fresh dates before.

"Delicious, aren't they? Well, then, so that's what brought me to Nizwa. And what a surprise! Nizwa actually *did* have this little toe in international drug trafficking, which I stumbled on and have faithfully kept secret from all of my employers. Nizwa is the home of the gentleman you met, Shaykh Zakariya Pahlavani, the *murshid*—you know some Arabic, don't you? *murshid*? guide?—anyway, the Supreme Guide of the Pahlavaniya Sufi brotherhood. Shaykh Zack—I call him Shaykh Zack—deals dope through his followers and has connections all over the world."

"Why did he shoot me? Everything I told him was true. I didn't have the violin."

"Ah, so you really don't have the violin! Oh, there's so many things we have to get to! So much to do. Pack all my things. Make up some wonderful stories to explain to all of my employers why I have to take some leave. It's going to be a busy two weeks."

"I don't understand," said Castle.

"My dear, of course you don't understand. How could you understand? You aren't even on square one yet. You've just seen a few of the pieces on the gameboard. There are rules we have to get through—penalty cards, how much a house costs, a hotel."

Castle was vaguely reminded of Pansy. "I don't want to understand. I just want to go home. And before that I want to telephone so I don't lose my job. I just finished a month out of the office while I was on jury duty, and two extra weeks off without telling anyone will just—"

Anderson fixed him with a look of somber gravity tinged with derision. "Your job, Mr. Winter, is not part of the game. Forget it. Until we leave, here you will remain, safely hidden away from any telephones."

"Until we leave?"

"I'm going with you."

"Is that necess—" Castle stopped short in embarrassment. "I don't mean I'm not very grateful for your saving me."

"I saved you because I was indirectly responsible for your being shot. Shaykh Zack proposed a mission for me, and I refused. He said he could force me. I said he couldn't. It turns out he could. He and Zaid, his chief disciple, shot you just to pose a dilemma for me. Either I didn't rescue you, in which case you would have died because the fort is closed, and only the Pahlavanis, and I, knew you were being brought there. Or I did rescue you, in which case I would have to explain everything to you, and you would make all kinds of trouble for me when you got home. Given that a dead American in my territory would have been a profound embarrassment for me and the DEA, my only recourse was to agree to Shaykh Zack's mission. So as painful as it will be for both of us, I am going to return to the United States with you and prove to you why you must keep your little adventure in Oman a secret. And you, out of your deep gratitude for all I have done, will help me do a little job."

Castle had lined up ten long, thin date stones on the edge of the table. He concentrated on flicking them with his middle finger across the room. After the fifth stone he said, "I could just promise not to say anything." Then he thought of what Pansy would think of someone who refused to help on a Sufi shaykh's mission. When he had flicked the tenth stone, he looked up. Anderson's creased, ruined face was set in a mordant grimace. "What. . . ?"

"My dear, I thought you would never ask. Our mission is two-fold: to recover Shaykh Zack's violin, and to kill Moosa Makki."

10

John Anderson was seated on a rush mat clad in the flowing white robes of a Nigerian gentleman. His audience was propped up in bed with a borrowed Malay sarong wrapped around his waist.

"Castle, my dear, I am going to tell you a story of how the real world really works . . .

"The story begins with Bashir. There are thousands of Bashirs in the Gulf. Let's imagine Bashir is an alert, bespectacled young fellow with a pleasant manner and some training in bookkeeping. It doesn't really matter, because Bashir is just a person, and people count for very little in stories of how the real world really works.

"Bashir starts as a bright and ambitious village boy in Pakistan. He wants to give money to his father and mother who sacrificed so he could go to school and also get enough money ahead for himself so he can get married. He goes to a Pakistani overseas employment office and gets a job in the United Arab Emirates, the UAE—let us say in Sharjah—keeping the books of a company that imports videotapes. At the end of every month, the company pays him fifteen hundred dirhams. That's somewhere around five hundred dollars.

"Now, Pakistani law requires Pakistanis working in the Gulf countries to deposit any dirhams they wish to send home in a Pakistani bank. That way no one can evade taxes, and the government knows how much foreign exchange is entering the country. The worker's family can then withdraw an equivalent amount in rupees back in Pakistan. Now, if the rate of exchange is four to one, and Bashir spends five hundred dirhams every month on living expenses, he has one thousand dirhams left to send home. So his family, by law, should be able to withdraw four thousand rupees from a bank.

"But Bashir knows a prosperous *hoondi* in the bazaar named Zahid. 'Hoondi' is an Indian and Pakistani world for money-changer. Zahid the Hoondi is willing to give Bashir one thousand extra rupees for his one thousand dirhams, that is, five thousand instead of four thousand. Moreover, Zahid promises that the rupees will be delivered directly to Bashir's mother and father in their village. This will save them the time and expense of a trip to town. Pakistani friends in Sharjah tell Bashir that Zahid the Hoondi is as good as his word. So Bashir gives his dirhams to Zahid, and his father writes to say that the five thousand rupees have been delivered as promised.

"Zahid the Hoondi now has Bashir's one thousand United Arab Emirates dirhams. The dirham, unlike the rupee, is a strong currency because the UAE economy floats on oil like a cork on champagne. Zahid the Hoondi deposits his one thousand dirhams in a bank and writes a letter confirming the deposit to Mr. Ma, his associate in Hong Kong. Mr. Ma is an enterprising Chinese businessman. He promptly goes to the corresponding bank in Hong Kong, withdraws the money, and changes it to US dollars. Let us say Mr. Ma takes a bit of a beating on the exchange rate and only gets three hundred US dollars for his one thousand UAE dirhams.

"Mr. Ma takes his three hundred dollars to the Greater East Asian Household Electronics Wholesale Emporium and Video Arcade and buys, for sixty dollars each, three VCRs, manufactured with miraculous efficiency in Korea. He thus pays a total of one hundred eighty dollars. The remainder of the three hundred is spent on the various bribes and transport fees needed to get the VCRs to Pakistan without going through customs.

"Because Pakistan is a poor country, it does not wish to see its meager wealth disappear into the treasure vaults of efficient Korean VCR manufacturers. But because the Pakistan government does not wish to see its middle class discontented, and possibly even rebellious, there has to be a way to sate their insatiable appetite for Korean VCRs. Answer to dilemma? The Pakistani gray market.

"Now imagine a man named Shaheen coming in his little car to a dusty row of shops outside Peshawar. Shaheen has an American university degree. He works for the Ministry of Education because he doesn't want to leave his wife and children to toil in Saudi Arabia or the Gulf. He makes about as much per month as a hotel clerk in Sharjah, but that's a rather large amount by Pakistani standards. As cultured people with many experiences outside Pakistan, Shaheen and his wife yearn for the world of cultural richness a Korean VCR would make available to them.

"So after some haggling Shaheen buys one of the VCRs for thirty-six hundred rupees, or about three hundred dollars. The other VCRs sell to similar customers for the same price. Net result for Zahid the Hoondi, and Mr. Ma in Hong Kong? A two hundred percent profit.

"Note, now, that more or less everything that has taken place is normal business practice. There is a whole world of smuggling that operates this way, more or less, based on the paychecks of the huge number of foreign workers in the Gulf. But there is one remaining problem. Mr. Ma and Zahid the Hoondi, profit is in rupees. Mr. Ma, in particular, would take a big loss changing his rupees into a more useful currency.

"Wouldn't it be better if they could buy something in Pakistan that could be converted to hard currency elsewhere? Something like heroin, for example? Good idea. Poppies are the world's hardiest crop. The Afghans are growing them like mad and manufacturing heroin. It's readily available around Peshawar. So in this version of the story, Mr. Ma and Zahid the Hoondi's associate in Pakistan spend most of the profit from the VCRs, say six thousand rupees, to buy a kilo of heroin. He divides the heroin into five bags and pays five Pakistani travelers five hundred rupees each to conceal one bag in their luggage when they fly to the United States. Total investment: eighty-five hundred rupees.

"When the travelers clear customs in New York, a man named Ahmad meets them and relieves them of the heroin. Ahmad then sells the kilo of heroin to a wholesaler for one hundred thousand dollars, or one million, two hundred thousand rupees. He easily covers all of his costs and shares the handsome profits with Mr. Ma, Zahid the Hoondi, and their associate in Pakistan. Zahid's original investment of one thousand rupees, the premium he paid Bashir to get him to deposit his dirhams, has now multiplied almost twelve hundred times.

"But, of course, this is much more seriously illegal than what Zahid the Hoondi and Mr. Ma had originally done in taking advantage of a comparatively safe and long-established smuggling opportunity. Higher risks justify higher profits because a slip-up at any point along the way would permit the intrepid and vigilant agents of the United States Drug Enforcement Administration, who neither slumber nor sleep in their attention to their duties, to penetrate the conspiracy and roll it up.

"Now, pay close attention to this special version of the story. What if there was a special bond that held Zahid the Hoondi, Mr. Ma in Hong Kong, and everyone else along the line down to Ahmad in New York in so tight a grip that betrayal would be unthinkable? Supposing, for example, they were all devoted to a worldwide brotherhood that enjoined absolute obedience to a Supreme Guide? To a Muslim Sufi mystic order, for example."

Castle arranged his sarong about his legs for the fifteenth time and longed for the security of his Jockey shorts, which had been spirited away for washing. He had been paying close attention to Anderson's long tale. It raised certain questions.

"I think—"

"No need to say anything! I know what you are thinking. You're thinking: Could it possibly be true that a Sufi brotherhood, devoted to religious meditation and ritual, has followed this route and turned a little innocent smuggling into a worldwide drug business? Is it even conceivable that the Pahlavaniya, with its thousands of devotees spread from Karachi to Manila to New York to Istanbul to Baku, would hypocritically engage in such criminal activities? And how in the world could Shaykh Zakariya, the aged and pious *murshid* of the Pahlavaniya, to whom every member of the order owes absolute obedience, manage to pull the strings of this fantastic network from an obscure town in the center of Oman? Finally, most important of all, does this mean that the charmingly eccentric, but for all that rather dashing, undercover DEA agent in Nizwa is actually there to penetrate this insidious cult of dope dealers instead of to monitor the distribution of a nonexistent drug called Green Mountain Blue?"

"Well?" said Castle when it became evident that his turn had finally arrived.

"Yes and no," replied Anderson with a sigh. "Yes and no."

When Castle could walk a bit, they toured the date factory. The women workers wore identical blue print shawls as a kind of uniform.

"We were supposed to provide employment for Omani women to involve them in the modern world and free them from the mindless monotony of traditional life. As it happened, word got around quickly that working in the factory was the very essence of mindless monotony, and no Omani women would agree to work. So these women are mostly the wives of Pakistani or Egyptian foreign workers."

Castle found the machines in the factory fascinating to watch, as machines in factories so often were. Things scooted here and there on conveyors to be dried or weighed or shaped or packaged. But in the end? A box of dates, nothing more. Another suppressed sneeze from the virus of the Industrial Revolution.

They sat in the manager's office with the machines pantomiming modernity through the windows behind them. John Anderson looked the very model of an American advisor to the Third World in khaki pants, safari jacket, and heavy work shoes.

"I've been debating with myself how much you should know."

Castle hadn't seen Anderson for more than brief periods in several days. "I would have been happy to participate in the debate," he replied.

Anderson ignored Castle's attempt at banter. He opened the drawer of the manager's desk and took out several typed pages held together by a paperclip. "I've decided that you should know more about the violin. It's what I call a story about how the unreal world really works." He looked down at the papers and then handed them to Castle.

Every Sufi brotherhood traces its origin to some holy figure whom its members believe attained a mystical union with God. Each Sufi is the last link in a holy chain called a *silsila*. The master of the brotherhood guides his disciples along the stages of mystic experience until they attain union with God. The master certifies this, just as his master certified him, and his master was certified by a previous master, back to the founder of the brotherhood, who himself would trace his mystic chain back to Muhammad or Ali, or some other figure from Islam's earliest history. One great Sufi would give his name to a brotherhood for several generations, and then it might split, or develop suborders, when Sufis farther along the chain proclaimed some change in organization or in mystic practice.

Traditionally the master gave a patched cloak to each disciple who completed the stages of mystic ascent. The cloak, like everything else personally connected with the master, contained holy power called *baraka*. In some brotherhoods the master would reserve a special token, endowed with the most powerful *baraka*, for his favorite disciple, the one he wished to have succeed him.

Pir Muhammad Pahlavan, who founded the Pahlavaniya as an offshoot of the Mevleviya about three hundred and fifty years ago, gave such a special token to his successor even though his own master had not done so. The Mevlevis believed that rotating slowly for several hours while music played brought them closer to God. Pir Muhammad made the dance secondary and put the emphasis on the power of the music. History books name him as the most skilled oud player of his time, and his disciples declared that his music induced a state of bliss that was a foretaste of mystic union with God.

When Pir Muhammad was very old, he called his disciples around him. He announced that he was going to die, and then, in their presence, he smashed his favorite oud, which he had made himself. After that he bestowed a new oud upon his favorite disciple, a young Turk named Sulaiman Sivasli. Pir Muhammad never played again, but Sulaiman Sivasli, who had not previously been known as a great musician, proved capable of inducing the same kind of musical trance. His music was not as beautiful to ordinary listeners as Pir Muhammad's had been, but he became the master of the brotherhood.

After Sulaiman Sivasli, each master destroyed his own instrument when he passed on the leadership and gave a new one to his chosen successor. Each time the successor proved able to enthrall the Sufis with the music he made, even when he had not previously been highly trained in music. The reason, according to the Pahlavanis, is that Pir Muhammad had composed a powerful talisman that made the charmed instrument produce divine music when played by someone of sufficiently elevated spiritual attainment. They say that the charm is written inside the instrument where it can't be seen, and no one is able to read it. Each *murshid* writes the charm in the instrument he makes for his successor.

Another theory about the charm takes off from Pir Muhammad's epithet "Pahlavan." *Pahlavan*, or *pahlawan* in Arabic, is a Persian word meaning hero or champion. Usually it was used for an athlete or a warrior rather than a musician, but the Pahlavanis believe it was bestowed on Pir Muhammad in recognition of his excellence as a musician. On the other hand, they agree with the history books in believing that Pir Muhammad was a Jawi, which means someone from Java or, more generally, the islands of Southeast Asia. So the alternative theory is that Pir Muhammad actually came from the island of Palawan, which is in the Muslim part of the Philippines. His original name, then, should have been Pal-awani, but it was assimilated to the more familiar sounding Pahlavan.

The second theory might also explain the mystery of the charm that is said to be in a mystic, unreadable language. Possibly it is written in Pir Muhammad's native language from Palawan, and hence is unreadable only because Arabs, Persians, Turks, and other members of the order don't know that obscure tongue.

In support of the second theory is the fact that while the Pahlavaniya, like many other Sufi brotherhoods, has thousands of devotees scattered through many Muslim countries, it is the only brotherhood that has a large following among the Muslims of the Philippines. It is strong in other Southeast Asian countries as well.

Regardless of the exact nature of the charm, however, the *baraka*-laden musical instrument, for at least the past century no longer an oud but a violin, remains the symbol of authority of the master of the Pahlavaniya. Its theft in 1986, therefore, dealt a grievous blow to the master's authority and was a profoundly disturbing event for all Pahlavanis.

"That's as far as I've gotten." John Anderson squared the typed pages, reattached the paperclip, and put them back in the desk. "It's for *Aramco World*. I can't finish it until we find out what happened to the violin, but it tells you pretty much what you need to know about it. It should make a good article some day.

"Shaykh Zack, the poor thing, was making the new violin for his successor when the old one was stolen. He was going to copy the talisman just before giving the new violin to his successor and then immediately destroy the old violin. Zaid, the other man who shot you, is Shaykh Zack's designated successor. But now the whole brotherhood is threatened by a breakdown in absolute authority, and the thief, assuming he can play the violin right, might even try to take over the Pahlavaniya, or at least its drug network."

Castle had been listening with rapt attention to the violin mystery being unraveled. Pansy will be thrilled, he thought. "The thief, I assume, is this person Moosa Makki?"

"Well, my dear, that has to be the assumption. He and

81

two other Pahlavanis disappeared at the same time as the violin. Makki had made it clear he expected to succeed Shaykh Zack, but Shaykh Zack decided to bestow the new violin on Zaid instead. Moosa Makki couldn't bear losing so he sneaked the violin out of Shaykh Zack's room and disappeared. And, incidentally, Moosa Makki and the other two are reportedly all Americans."

"When did this happen?"

"Two years ago. I was on leave back in the States so it all took place while I was away. They say Moosa Makki was an extraordinarily gifted young man who could perform miracles. He came to Nizwa specifically to receive Shaykh Zack's blessing. He was here for only a short time, too short apparently to supplant loyal, humdrum Zaid in Shaykh Zack's affections. By the time I returned from leave, Makki was gone. I never saw him."

Castle's head was aswim with the painkillers he had been taking ever since leaving Nizwa. The trip through mountain and desert back to Musqat had passed in a haze. An officious Sikh had steered him through check-in procedures at Musqat airport and led him onto the plane. The Sikh was even now sitting beside the soft nest of pillows and blankets he and Castle had plumped up next to the window to minimize the pressure on Castle's dully throbbing thighs.

The Sikh had taken off his brown suitcoat and was sitting in his vest and white shirt reading the *International Herald Tribune*. His tightly wound turban, peaked above his forehead, was magenta, and he was wearing a kind of hairnet under his chin to keep his graying beard pressed close to his neck. His heavily lined face was grave and his eyes dark and penetrating as they scanned the headlines. He was, of course, John Anderson.

Fleeting portions of conversation registered disjointedly in Castle's mind. Anderson had adopted a thick Indian accent.

"Well, you see, then. That is how it is. I just wanted to

overturn every stone for you. Otherwise I should be feeling very guilty."

"What are you talking about," murmured Castle sleepily.

"Two hundred million dollars. Think of it. More than two hundred crores of rupees. All for the man with the violin. But where, one is wondering, is the violin? Perhaps your ladyfriend has it?"

Castle drifted off to sleep.

"The question, you see, is coming down to where is the violin?"

The bump of landing jarred Castle awake. He vaguely recalled lying stretched out on a stainless steel and foam rubber chair in the Frankfurt transit lounge. This, therefore, must be New York.

Home.

Like a crocus in March, Castle felt a stirring throughout his system. As passengers filed past he groggily released himself from his seatbelt, bundled the blankets and pillows into the empty seat beside him, and felt under the seat ahead for his shoes.

He did not see Anderson the Sikh at the baggage claim, and he did not look for him. Castle was home. With luck he would never see the weirdo Anderson again. His heart beat hard as he walked down the green-labeled aisle for travelers with nothing to declare.

"No luggage?" said the portly customs officer to a muscular young man with a Marine haircut standing ahead of Castle.

"San Francisco," mouthed the young man.

"You gotta get your luggage through customs here. Not San Francisco. Go back and get it." The young man looked momentarily murderous and then ambled off.

"Soldier. These are the guys who are supposed to protect us," said the official as he beckoned Castle forward. "Can't even read. What would they do in a war? I'm telling ya. No luggage?"

"No luggage."

"Where do you live?" He looked at the passport Anderson had given Castle at Musqat airport. "You coming from Oman with no luggage?"

"It got lost in Frankfurt. I live in New York. Upper West Side."

The official slapped the passport shut and handed it back. Castle walked through a glass door into JFK Airport, Queens, New York. He was home.

Elsewhere in Queens, in a one-room fourth-floor apartment with bedding on the floor and a hot plate on a small table by the window, a slight Dominican youth put a bow to the strings of a violin that showed dollops of white glue around its edges and at the base of its new bridge. The first passage of the bow brought forth a sound of ethereal beauty.

"Piece of cake," said Frankie.

11

A miniature staircase of mail descended halfway down Castle's long coffee table, leaving him room at the end for opening it. The highest step of the staircase was a pile of catalogs: Land's End, J. Crew, L.L. Bean, Brookstone Hard-to-Find Tools, Macy's, Eddie Bauer, Early Winters, Voice of the Mountains, On the Run. Castle didn't believe in mail-order purchasing, but he could never bring himself just to throw mail away. Judith had been the one with the craving for catalogs. Castle had regarded it as an expensive but tolerable addiction. Only after Judith left did he discover that death alone could remove a person's name and address from the catalog houses' mailing lists.

The next highest step was Judith's legacy, too: solicitations for welfare reform, immigration reform, abortion rights, conservation of wilderness, protection of threatened fauna, and preservation of endangered members of congress. Step three down contained subscribed-to magazines: *The New Yorker, Scientific American, The Economist;* step four: bills, bank statements, insurance premium notices, "important tax documents." Finally, a precious stack of four genuine letters, addressed by hand, sealed by tongue, stamped by thumb, and personally delivered in a leather pouch by a U.S. Postal Service letter carrier in nostalgic re-creation of a dimly remembered American custom.

Castle's employer wrote a warm personal note to inform him officially of the termination of his employment.

The other three were from Pansy.

Tuesday, February 2

Dear Castle,

In a text adventure the sudden disappearance of a companion with whom one is questing can arise from death, magic displacement, a curse, the companion being actually a figment of one's imagination, or, very rarely, from some fault or lack in his equipment or preparation for the quest. If you have left home for one of these reasons, I hope the problem is temporary and you will find your way back. I truly do.

You'll laugh at something I found out. My father had a friend who was in the army in Japan after World War II and married a Japanese woman. The Japanese didn't drink milk or eat dairy products then. I don't know if they do now or not. She said that she loved her husband even though he smelled like butter! It wasn't his eating meat, you see. It was his drinking milk. I remembered it all wrong!

Love,
Pansy

Castle carried the letter to his kitchenette and reread it while he opened a can of devilled ham and made himself a sandwich. He read the next letter while he ate it.

Thursday, February 4

Dear Castle,

It is true, as you must know by now, that I have despised you in my heart for abandoning me. Ours need not have been a fleeting romance. I could have changed my entire life for you. Even better, I could have changed your entire life. Do not try to find me. I have left my apartment. The great Mamadou came looking for me, but I escaped her clutches.

Love lost,
Pansy

The third letter, like the others, was postmarked New York City.

Dear Castle,

All is forgiven! I have fled to a distant part. Mamadou is still seeking me. If all is lost, 'twas lost in fashion grand!

I am changing in subtle ways, Castle. There was a time when I laughed at "The Real Pirate's Handbook." I suppose you have never heard of it. It was posted several years ago in various forms on electronic bulletin boards. I don't suppose you know what those are either. It listed the personal qualities computer software pirates thought of as being part of their true soul. You know what one of them was? "Real pirates are over fifteen." Can you grasp that? That means there are people UNDER FIFTEEN who not only know enough to break the protection codes on copyrighted software, but are good enough at it to be threatening to the over-fifteens. I know that you have no idea what I am talking about. The import of it, though, is that I have suddenly realized that by virtue of my age I am closer to you in ignorance than I am to the true computer generation in knowledge. So I am giving up my career in computers.

"Grow old, therefore, with me; the best is yet to be."

Love renewed,
Pansy

"'Along with,'" said Castle aloud angrily, "'grow old along with me; the best is yet to be.' For Christ's sake, get it right! Witless, half-educated . . ." He wadded up the letters and threw them in the wastebasket.

An hour later, after a second sandwich, he unwadded the letters and smoothed them out. What, exactly, had Pansy meant to say in the part about butter and being a vegetarian?

A new letter arrived three days later. It was postmarked Smart's Rock, Massachusetts.

Thursday, February 20

Dear Castle,

I know you have returned. I do not wish to deepen the guilt you are feeling over leaving the burden of our quest entirely upon my shoulders, but there are things I must tell you.

When I realized that you had cravenly abandoned your mission of deciphering the message in the violin, I pondered what to do. It occurred to me that the answer might lie with the other people who tried to claim the violin at the police station. You will remember the incredibly helpful and remarkably virile Assistant District Attorney Oshinsky who helped me previously. By good fortune, he again proved willing to assist in our quest. I was able to identify Mamadou Mustafa in a police scrapbook. Her name is Estelle Marie Whitehead: four arrests for drug possession with intent to sell, all dismissed after she proved helpful. Estelle Marie rented the apartment the violin was found in and lived there with her boyfriend Arnold Muhammad Mustafa. Arnold Muhammad was murdered on the street a couple of weeks before the grand jury hearing. Sidney and Thaddeus Monroe, who were the people arrested in the bust, are Estelle Marie's cousins. My guess is that Arnold Muhammad reported the violin stolen to be sure of eventually getting it back even if Sidney and Thaddeus were sent to jail. After he was killed, Mamadou tried to claim it in his name.

I did not look up Estelle Marie since I have reason to believe she is still angry at me for giving her a substitute violin, which I bought in a pawnshop. She and two men I think were Sidney and Thaddeus tried to attack me, but more of that anon.

The tall black man I mentioned to you, who called himself Muhammad Mustafa, was also in Mr. Oshinsky's scrapbook. Six arrests for narcotics possession and sale, and possessing an unlicensed handgun; served three years in prison; most recently picked up but not held as a suspect in the shooting of Arnold Muhammad. He was born Eldee or L.D. Germaine, but he became a Muslim and changed his name to Ali Abdussalam. My theory about him is that he knew Mamadou's boyfriend had stolen the violin, then lost it in the bust, then reported it stolen from him. So he was at the police station posing as Arnold Muhammad Mustafa. That's probably why he and Mamadou seemed to hate each other.

Mr. Oshinsky got me Ali Abdussalam's latest address—102nd near West End Avenue, not too far from you—so I went by the building. It had TV cables hanging from the roof so I called the cable company and ordered service to be installed at Ali's apartment number. They said fine. That told me that the apartment was either vacant, or Ali didn't get cable. So I asked if I could just have the account switched from the name Ali Abdussalam, whom I was taking over the apartment from. They said that was impossible because Ali Abdussalam had terminated his service.

I know you must be proud of my ingenuity, but I fear that telling you how well I have done will deepen your own sense of ineptitude and failure.

Here's the text, then. Arnold Muhammad and Mamadou steal the violin from Ali Abdussalam to sell it to somebody mysterious for $100,000. Ali tracks them to New York. Before he can get it back from them or they can sell it, the police confiscate it. While they're all waiting for the grand jury and Sidney and Thaddeus's trial, Ali and Arnold get into a fight, and Ali kills Arnold. Therefore, Ali is the one who is most likely to know what the violin message says. So my job turns out to be to find Ali.

I thought of a dozen clever ways to find out where he had moved. The easiest was paying the super $30 to find out from the realty company his forwarding address. It's 6 Sixth Road, Smart's Rock, Massachusetts.

As I pen these words, I am looking at 6 Sixth Road here in Smart's Rock, which is actually just part of Marshland, Massachusetts. It's not like the other houses around here, which are mostly shingle-sided summer places. We're only a block from the ocean. It's an old red brick bungalow with a nice little front porch with white wooden pillars. I have just rented an apartment across the street at 5 Sixth Road. So far I have discovered that Ali Abdussalam, who must be Smart's Rock's only black, worked for DJones Chemical Supply Company before he went to New York and has now come back. But I haven't seen him yet personally.

Now, dear Castle, I offer you a chance to redeem yourself. Join me here in my little apartment by the sea. With me as your companion, come and penetrate the unknown!

> With warmth and affection,
> Pansy

How, thought Castle, could a woman addicted to reading romance novels sound so literate? And how could a woman who sounded so literate close a letter with such a crude double entendre? Or was it simply crude of him to see it as a double entendre? Or did she deliberately make it seem like a too-crude double entendre so that he would feel guilty about suspecting her of such crudity?

*   *   *

The really hard thing about separation and divorce, Castle learned over the next few days, was taxes—prorating deductions for state taxes, division of charitable contributions, whose medical expenses were whose—endless considerations that all had to be quantified and explained in a memorandum demanded of him by Judith's lawyer. Then, after keyboarding the document into the computer, came the problem of formatting: how to get the columns to line up correctly on the print-out. Castle divided his time between a tome entitled *You, Your Divorce, and Money* and his word processing manual. As the hours slowly turned into days, the pain in his thighs almost disappeared. He pushed Pansy Garden out of his mind as he had previously done with John Anderson.

A doorbell buzz startled him so badly he hit the CLEAR key on his calculator and lost a total it had taken him an hour to arrive at. Through the brass peephole he saw a short youth with tight curly hair. Castle tried to think whether he had ordered some delivery.

"Who is it?" he said through the door.

"Yo! It's me, Frankie."

"Are you delivering?"

"No. Friend of Pansy's. She say come see you."

"What about?"

"Ticket to Boston for you."

"I'm not going to Boston."

"Not my problem, man. Come on, open the door and take the ticket."

"You keep it."

"You talkin' about? Pansy bust my ass I don't give you this ticket."

"Go away. I'm not going to Boston."

"You some tight-ass, you know that? Won't even open the door. Pansy never tell you about her friend Frankie?"

Castle peered through the peephole lens but didn't reply.

"She say if you don't take the ticket to say you still smell

90

like butter. And she say Mamadou is after her, and her little finger been cut off. You got that?"

Castle held his breath. Whose little finger? There was a hiss at his feet as an envelope whistled under the door and came to a stop against the little Persian rug in his foyer. Castle watched the slim youth saunter back down the hallway toward the elevator. "I'm not going to Boston!" he called again through the door, but not loudly enough to be heard.

Pansy, of course, was a nut, a complete fruitcake, mused Castle. Made things up, that was the key to her problem. Too many computer games. She had started living them. It was very sad because she probably wasn't even too illiterate by comparison with her age group. Notice how she said she was going to tell more about an "attack" by Mamadou Mustafa, alias Estelle Marie Whitehead, and two other villains "anon" but never got around to it. Probably wore her imagination out thinking up the other stuff. And after saying the butter smell thing was a joke to have Frankie refer to it.

She couldn't have made up the finger, though. Must be Mamadou's finger. Only Mr. Osman and he knew about that. So she must have at least seen Mamadou. Probably with a bandage.

A static-beset public address voice interrupted Castle's reverie.

"New Haven. The station stop is New Haven. Passengers for the inland route through Hartford to Boston should be in the front three cars. Passengers taking the coastal route through New London and Providence to Boston should be in the rear four cars. The station stop is New Haven."

12

The black-on-gray tracery of a snow-free winter forest gave way to flat purplish expanses of dormant cranberry bog as the turnoff from Route 3A meandered through the small coastal towns along Boston's South Shore before entering Marshland, Massachusetts. Castle maneuvered his rented Nissan carefully, on the lookout for some sign of or to the center of town. An unconvincingly perky blond teenager in a pink and white donut-selling uniform told him that Marshland had several small business districts separated by inlets and marshes. Really! Smart's Rock was a beach area with a lot of summer homes that were boarded up in winter. Castle couldn't miss it if he looked for the submarine tower.

Castle drove in the direction indicated reflecting on whether "submarine tower" was a contradiction in terms or whether people actually had built towers under the ocean, and if so, for what purpose. The donut girl had made it clear that what she really meant was a World War II concrete submarine lookout tower, but Castle was ready to grasp at any idle thought rather than reexamine the dozen or so completely persuasive arguments against his pursuing Pansy Garden to Smart's Rock, or anywhere else. His mind perversely rejected any distraction. Sex-starved, middle-aged, out of work, divorced, lonely, too dumb to see that he was being made a fool of. But then, why had he been shanghaied to Oman and shot? In his whole life he had done nothing that could provoke any rational person to even point a gun at him, and here he was with a white scar on the back of each thigh and a vestigial ache whenever he sat down. It simply made no sense. Pansy made no sense. John Anderson, wherever he had disappeared to, made no sense.

The submarine tower rose starkly on the horizon, a plain, rectangular, concrete silhouette seventy feet tall with three wide horizontal slits toward the top on its seaward side. The street signs changed from names to numbered roads. Sixth Road was a block-long dead end leading from the main street, directly across from Pat and Arthur's Restaurant, to the seawall. Beyond the wall was the cold, steely Atlantic. Five Sixth Road was a large frame building covered with tan aluminum siding. It looked too large to have ever been a private home, too houselike to have been built as an apartment building, and too new to have formerly been a barn. The main street merged with no curb into a more private-looking asphalt parking area in front of the unpainted wood porch that ran across the building's front. White doors were numbered 1 and 2.

Pansy had not mentioned an apartment number in her letter. Castle stepped silently to the window of apartment 2 and looked in. A genial-looking old man was smoking a pipe and reading a book in a recliner. A large television set dominated the cluttered but homey room. Castle tiptoed to the other door and pushed the buzzer.

"Castle!" screamed Pansy in delight the moment she threw open the door. She wrapped her arms around him in an impetuous embrace and kissed him long and lasciviously on the lips. All of the arguments against traveling to Boston vanished from his mind. "Castle, come in. I'm so happy to see you."

"I'm happy to see you, too, Pansy," replied Castle in carefully controlled understatement.

"I want you to say hello to John."

"John?"

Pansy stood back from the door and beckoned Castle inside. John Anderson, in a gray three-piece business suit, was standing in the archway to the kitchen across the narrow living room.

"My dear, you look as though you thought you would never see me again. How are your legs?"

"I hoped I would never see you again. What are you doing here?"

"John's living here and we're conspiring together," interjected Pansy, squeezing her shoulders together in excitement. "It's just like a text adventure. John's changed my whole life. He's so smart! He suggested having Frankie tell you about Mamadou's finger as a way to get you here."

Castle gazed coldly at the mismatched couple: Pansy a picture of punkish allure with her black lips, shaven temples, ragged sweatpants, and torn sweatshirt biased to reveal an enticingly bare right shoulder; John the image of a successful businessman with his gravely creased face and wisps of blond hair sweeping across his balding scalp. Castle exited without a word, tripped quickly down the porch steps, and started the car. He paused momentarily to reconsider, shuddered, and then drove off.

He angrily reconsidered his situation at greater length over a Pepsi Cola in a motel room a mile away on Ocean Avenue. Pansy had deceived him to get him to Boston. John had betrayed him by using the information he had confided to him in Oman to find Pansy and then conspire with her to get him to Boston. All that was clear. But the reason behind it was all unfathomable. What the situation amounted to was that Castle could return to New York, never see either of them again, never get kidnapped or shot at again, find a new job, meet a nice woman, lead the quiet life he longed for . . . and never find out what the whole thing was about. Or he could ask the obvious questions and take the risk of being drawn more deeply, and possibly dangerously, into something he might never understand.

In a dramatic and decisive gesture he crushed the aluminum can in his hand and reached for the telephone.

"Pansy? It's Castle. I'm just going to listen. If you can

explain to me in a rational way why I should come back, I'll come back."

"Darling, how wonderful!"

"One more thing. Don't 'darling' me unless you intend to get serious on the . . . the . . . personal level. I'm too old to try to guess at your affections by pulling the petals off flowers."

"Well, of course I intend to make wild, passionate, naked, sweating love with you someday, Castle. Just not real soon. I want to catch you when you're awake."

"Just what is that supposed to mean?"

"I thought you were going to keep quiet and listen to a rational explanation of things."

Castle ground his teeth. "I'm listening."

"John works for the Drug Enforcement Administration."

"I know that."

"You're supposed to be just listening. John found me because you told him about me, and he told me about your horrible experience in Oman and what that cruel old man did to you. You are incredibly brave!"

"Did he tell you about his adolescent houseboy?"

"John is on a mission. He must destroy an evil man named Moosa Makki and retrieve the Sufi violin. He told me that as long as Moosa Makki is at large or alive, whoever has the violin will never be safe."

"You told me you returned the violin to the police, but apparently you didn't."

"No, that was a lie. I didn't want you to worry."

"Then where is it?"

"Why, Castle, you sound just like John. Do you think for a moment I would tell a soul in the world where that violin is as long as Moosa Makki is scouring the country for it? I wouldn't be safe and neither would the person I told. That's why we have to help John destroy Moosa Makki. So we can live happily ever after. It's simple. Pure text adventure."

Castle considered. "All right," he vouchsafed after a long pause. "I'll be back in ten minutes."

"Where are you calling from?"

"The Anchor Asway Motel. It's very near you."

"Don't check out. There's only room for the two of us in this apartment, and you'll have to have a separate address to go to work from."

"Go to what work?" said Castle into the suddenly dead phone.

Pansy had persuaded a neighbor who was caretaking a summer house to lend her the owner's aluminum porch furniture. The bright green webbing of the seats clashed with the rust orange wall-to-wall carpeting. Castle could see a pile of jumbled bedding on the floor of the bedroom beyond the kitchen. A rectangular window, cut through the wall between the living room and the kitchen to the right of the connecting archway, made the small apartment seem more spacious.

John Anderson had changed into jeans and an *I Love the Sultan of Oman* T-shirt with the Sultan's picture on it. He leaned forward, elbows on knees, and fixed Castle with a sincere and entreating gaze.

"DJones Chemical Supply Company has its offices in that tall concrete building you saw coming here. The company is a contract supplier of drugs to the U.S. Army. The army has three laboratories that experiment with and keep track of narcotics, hallucinogens, and other sorts of drugs. The laboratories have two missions: to determine what effects different drugs might have on U.S. soldiers who encounter them in foreign countries, and to determine what use, if any, the army might make of them as weapons against possible enemies.

"Originally the army simply bought samples and experimented with volunteers. But the number of drug types has become much greater now, and our famous war on drugs is headline news. Consequently, the army decided it had to enlarge its operation but, at the same time, became concerned that it might get a black eye if some major got busted in Turkey buying heroin for Uncle Sam.

"So they decided to contract it out. DJones employees buy specified amounts of drugs all over the world, bring them into the country, and sell them to the U.S. Army. This is all on the up-and-up. They have formal exemption from all Drug Enforcement Administration oversight. The submarine tower they use as a headquarters is army property on a dollar-a-year lease. You following?"

"It's not too hard," replied Castle coldly.

"Okay, good. So that's DJones Company, the army, and the DEA. Now we come to the GAO, the General Accounting Office, which is the agency of Congress that looks into how the taxpayers' money is being spent. Congressman Francis X. Malone, who represents this district, received an anonymous complaint that DJones Chemical Supply Company was abusing its special status and collaborating with corrupt army officers to bring in large quantities of drugs in addition to the ones they were selling the army.

"Malone didn't even know DJones Company worked for the army, and he was furious when he found out. So he ordered the GAO to investigate. GAO called DEA to ask them what was what, but DEA told them they didn't know anything because they had a written agreement to keep out of DJones's affairs. GAO responded that they didn't feel they could handle the investigation properly without DEA assistance because no one but DEA had the kind of information on commodity prices and routes of supply that the investigators would need. So-o-o-o . . . DEA said they would supply a liaison person to supply the necessary expertise on condition that that person abide by DEA's agreement with the army and remain only a passive resource for GAO's own investigator. My dear, would you believe that I am DEA's liaison man? And that you—"

"I think I see where this is heading," interrupted Castle, "and the answer is no."

John threw up his hands. "Ah! Turning down the opportunity of a lifetime. I refuse to believe it. You're a smart man, old boy. Moreover, you have keen intuition. I've said so to Pansy, haven't I, Pansy?"

"John thought it was brilliant the way you figured out where the violin was from."

"All you have to do is go to work for a few days with DJones as a General Accounting Office investigator, just until you can find out who in the company, if anyone, is Moosa Makki. Then I can take him to a cranberry bog and shoot holes in him or do one of those other picturesque DEA things. But I can't set foot on the premises of DJones Company myself because I'm DEA, and we have our agreement with the army. I want Moosa Makki, but I'm not going to lose my job over him."

"Bullshit!" exploded Castle. "This is just a lot of bullshit! I don't believe a word you're telling me. I can't say I'm from the General Accounting Office. I don't have any identification, and I don't have the slightest idea what a GAO investigator would do. What would he investigate? If they showed me the books, I wouldn't know what I was looking for."

"Well, my dear, of course you wouldn't. No one's asking you to be a real investigator. This is all just eyewash for DJones. There's no real investigation. We're just telling DJones that there is. I wrote a letter, a very, very, official-looking DEA letter—in fact, I suppose, a genuinely official DEA letter—to Donald Jones, who's the president of DJones Chemical Supply Company, saying that Mr. John Winter—that sounds a lot more accountantlike than Castle Winter, don't you think?—of the GAO will be arriving to review their supply and inventory control systems. Then I telephoned him from Washington and told him that the object of the investigation is not DJones but the army itself so he shouldn't say a word about this to his army contacts."

"Donald Jones has one letter and one phone call, and you expect him on the basis of that to show me around his tower? If I were he, I would be on the phone to Congressman Malone as soon as I read the letter."

"You would if you were an honest businessman. But if Donald Jones is Moosa Makki, or one of Makki's disciples, he isn't an honest businessman. My guess is that he's really doing exactly what I suggested to you in Oman, using this business, and the authority he can claim among the Pahlavanis from having the violin, to steal part of the Pahlavaniya drug smuggling operation from Shaykh Zack. The company is ostensibly very small so it has to act as if it can't afford to lose its army contract. Logic dictates, therefore, that they should welcome a government audit. Furthermore, in gratifying response to the dictates of logic, I have received a reply from Donald Jones saying that Mr. Winter would be more than welcome to look over his operation."

"And be arrested for fraud and impersonation as soon as he shows his face," snarled Castle.

"Perhaps. Pansy and I haven't noticed any police around, though. What it boils down to, old sport, is that either you take a risk and infiltrate DJones Company, or you leave poor, dear Pansy never knowing when Moosa Makki will find her and force her to hand over the violin. And my goodness, what agony she might have to endure if that ever happened."

"**P**ansy and I haven't noticed any police around," repeated Castle prissily as he drove back to the Anchor Asway with a letter of introduction on DEA stationery on the seat beside him. "You and Pansy. Pansy and John. Pansy and pansy. Kidnapped, shot. Now I'm going to break the law because of that . . ." His angry voice trailed off in the empty car. He recalled Pansy's good-bye to him on the porch.

"I can't believe you're living with him, Pansy," he'd said. "Everything he says sounds phony. Moreover, he's as gay as a Greenwich Village drag queen."

"No, he isn't. It's just his manner. I think it's kind of cute. Besides, your homophobia is revolting, disgusting, and a sign of great immaturity and self-doubt."

"Cute, bullshit! If he's pretending he's heterosexual, I can assure you it's only an act."

"But what an actor!" replied Pansy with a sigh. "Last night he gave a rock solid performance three hours long." She smiled beatifically. "Good-bye, Castle."

"I don't believe you!" shouted Castle now as he passed under the leaning anchor sign of the Anchor Asway Motel and guided his car to space 14.

13

On the Sixth Road side, access to the submarine tower was through a gap between the tower's chain-link fence and the unpainted picket fence of a neighbor's driveway. The chain-link fence and the seawall enclosed a triangular area of gravel, weeds, and scattered trash some seventy feet deep. A vehicle gate opened onto the gravel from Fifth Road, and a small house trailer with a sign saying DJONES CHEMICAL SUPPLY COMPANY on its side was parked just inside the gate, a few feet from the tower. Beside the trailer was a blue Pontiac.

Castle looked up at the tower. It was about twelve feet on each side, and he recalled having been told that it was seventy-some feet high. Three concrete steps with iron pipe railings led to the single entrance, a narrow door on the side facing the sea. Up to about fifty feet, the only other features were the faint impressions of wooden forms and a tiny seaward window at the halfway level. Toward the top were three floors marked by slot windows, surmounted by sloping concrete awnings about a foot deep that stretched the building's full width. A windscreen, seemingly made of black plastic panels, surrounded the flat roof. Above it Castle could see two antennas.

"John Winter, General Accounting Office," replied Castle

to a query from the intercom speaker set in the doorframe above the buzzer.

"Come on up," said the thin telephonic voice.

The door buzzed; Castle pushed. There was nothing before him but a concrete stairway. By the time he finally reached a door after almost a hundred steps he was thoroughly winded. The man who opened the door had orange hair going gray at the temples, a long arched nose that emphasized the length of his face, and white bushy eyebrows that seemed to be unraveling into tangled threads. He appeared to be about Castle's age and was dressed similarly in a blue business suit.

"I'm John Winter. I'm from the General Accounting Office. This letter—"

"No problem, Mr. Winter," said the man good-naturedly, waving aside the letter. "We're pleased to have you here. I'm Donald Jones. Come on inside. Let me get out of your way. The doorways in this building are very narrow."

The room was eleven feet square with one walled-off corner. A sink was visible through its partly open door. The concrete walls were painted yellow and ornamented with maps of different regions of the world. Two metal desk were situated to provide views out the foot-high window that ran the length of the seaward wall. A dark skinny man with thinning black hair and dark-rimmed glasses was puffing a pipe behind a desk with a personal computer on it.

"This is Mr. Maghee," said Jones, gesturing to the skinny man. "Moe, this is John Winter. He'll be with us for a while. General Accounting Office. I told you about it." The skinny man knocked his pipe against the heel of his hand, deposited the dottle in an ashtray, and balanced the pipe in the groove on the edge of the ashtray before slowly easing his chair back, standing up, and silently proffering a bony hand. Short but not quick, thought Castle. "I'm sure Mr. Winter will be asking you what you do eventually." To Castle he continued, "Mr. Maghee manages our inventory control system. You will discover that he is very precise. As you can imagine, we have to be accountable for every gram of substance we import. But you'll find out all about that later. Follow me up-stairs. That's where I have my office."

The upstairs walls were painted green. A shaggy woven hanging that abstractly conveyed an outdoorsy feeling covered the wall opposite the slit window. Below it was a brown leather sofa. Castle wondered how they had gotten it up the stairs. At a right angle to the sofa was a dark brown Formica-topped desk. Behind the desk was a metal bookcase, full of what looked like catalogues, and a luxurious swivel chair. In front of it was a visitor's chair with upholstered seat and arms. Castle took the latter seat while Donald Jones settled into the former.

Castle had worked his speech out in advance. Donald Jones listened gravely and attentively. He declared firmly that he personally would tolerate neither evasion, nor deception, nor concealment, nor malfeasance on the part of his employees in the assistance he would order them to render to Mr. Winter of the GAO. Castle weighed Jones's tone of voice and facial expression to see whether they accorded with him being either an international drug dealer, a deceitful Sufi mystic, or both. He concluded that Mr. Jones put him most in mind of a confident small businessman forthrightly promising to do his best to cooperate with a tax auditor to prove himself above suspicion.

"Keep in mind, Mr. Winter, that we are actually a very small operation here in the United States. The army issues a substance request, specifying the amount needed, on a substance request form. Depending on the part of the world indicated, we communicate the request to our extensive network of finders. They report back, in a code we use to protect our sources, on possible suppliers and prices, quality and purity standards, reliability, mode of purchase, and so forth."

"I take it most of the substances you buy are not legally for sale even in the source country."

"Quite right. That, of course, is why the U.S. Army can't simply send uniformed officers to the neighborhood Colombian substance store to buy some substance."

"So your sources are drug dealers . . ."

"It is company policy to call them substances. Just a technicality."

". . . and your finders are people with extensive drug underworld connections."

"Yes. Contacts in the substance marketing community. But I must mention, because it is something we are very proud of, that our finders, unlike many of our suppliers, are people of absolute loyalty and honesty. It's almost like a bond between them and the company. Their reliability is what enables us to fulfill our contracts."

"What kind of bond do you mean?"

"Well, just sort of a bond bond. It's a manner of speaking."

"Still, quite extraordinary. I mean, I don't suppose loyalty and honesty are all that widespread in the substance marketing community. How did you establish your finders' network? I suppose you have a list of people who are part of it."

"Of course there's a list. But it's coded and proprietary. As for how the network was established, I didn't personally do it. I just came to know of its existence and thought of a way to utilize it commercially. Up until two years ago I was marketing vice president of a small company in Cupertino that manufactured special kinds of computer chips."

"How did you make the change?"

Jones stood up and beckoned Castle to the concrete stairway. "Come on up to the roof. You must see the view."

Castle followed him up. They passed through the next floor, this one painted blue and furnished with a single bed, dresser, chair, table, microwave oven, and miniature refrigerator. "I live here," said Jones over his shoulder as he started up the final flight of stairs. "I have a passion for towers. We rent this one for a dollar a year from the army to use as an office, and I didn't see any reason why I shouldn't just live here." Sunlight and cold air flooded down from above as Jones opened the door to the roof. Castle followed him outside into an icy gale roaring over the black plastic windscreen panels.

"Windy today," shouted Jones over the roar. His bold stance and orange hair flying in the wind put Castle in mind of a pirate captain astride his poop deck. "God, how I love a tower." Jones stretched his arms out and joyously filled his lungs. Castle was freezing. "Smart's Rock's rock itself is directly out from us." Jones pointed. "There's an iron stairway down from the seawall there at the end of the lot. See the breakwater beyond it? Like those other breakwaters north and south? They stop beach erosion. Up to about three-quarters of the way out, this one here is made from boulders that were barged in. Then where the color gets lighter it merges with a big outcropping of natural rock. That's Smart's Rock. All the other breakwaters are completely artificial. Those cliffs up to the north are in Ocean Bluff. South of us is Green Harbor."

And east, thought Castle, is England, with nothing in between. The tiny figure of a person stepping carefully amidst the jumbled boulders out toward Smart's Rock reminded him of how high up he was, and he suddenly remembered to be frightened. "It's cold up here," he said with a shiver in his voice. He turned around and went back down the stairs.

Pansy's mane flew out in a tail behind her in the fierce wind. She squinted into it and planted her foot firmly before entrusting her weight to the next boulder. She had walked the white beach from First Road down to the Smart's Rock breakwater without encountering a single person. But her mind's eye had filled the landscape with the characters and equipment she considered appropriate to a drug smuggling operation: a rubber boat with an outboard motor up on the sand being emptied of wooden crates by men dressed in black wet suits; a speedboat killing its engine and drifting toward shore being met by other men wading into the water to receive its valuable cargo; a helicopter with strangely silent rotors swooping in low from the sea to land on the gravel lot in front of the submarine tower. She looked back at the tower silhouetted against the sky and imagined signals being flashed to secret watchers from its slit windows and coded radio messages being beamed out to sea from its antennas.

The jump down from the last boulder onto the smoother surface of Smart's Rock proper threatened not so much injury as the possibility of landing in a big gooey mass of gelatinous seaweed and flotsam. One bulging blue portion of the mass looked disgustingly like a drowned person. Pansy looked again and decided not to jump at all. The bulging blue mass half shrouded in the greenish-brown weed *was* a drowned person, wedged into a deep crevice of rock.

Pansy's eye sorted out the bumps and twists and found the dark head pointed downward with its face in the foamy water. It was Mamadou Musafa, a.k.a. Estelle Marie Whitehead.

I saw a person today who could have made me a million dollars if I had asked her the right question, thought Pansy, but I didn't. "Have a nice day," she said weakly through a constricted throat. She turned and picked her way slowly back across the boulders.

"Not the slightest bit of trouble," boasted Castle to a two-person audience in a high-backed booth at Pat and Arthur's Restaurant. "He never had the slightest suspicion that I wasn't from the GAO. Going to let me see everything. Though I'm not sure how much there is to see. Jones lives there. Maghee works there. And there's a third desk. But I don't see how a place that small could have many more workers. Of course, there's a trailer outside."

"What's in the rest of the building?" asked John Anderson, who was paying much closer attention than Pansy, who seemed distracted.

"Nothing, I guess. I mean, there isn't really a rest of the building. You come in, and there's a stairway, nothing else. No landing or doorway or anything until you get to the top."

"It must be hollow outside the stairwell, though. No one would build a tower that thick out of solid concrete."

"Well, I suppose you're right," said Castle, sipping his Pepsi.

"What about Maghee?"

"Dark, wiry little guy, big glasses. Sort of like a miniature owl. Slow and deliberate."

"Does he have an accent?"

"Maybe. Sort of. Nothing I could place."

Pansy interrupted. "I ran into someone today who could have changed all of our lives if I had asked the right question," she said solemnly. "But I didn't do it."

"Who was that?" asked John.

"Mamadou Musafa, also known as Estelle Marie Whitehead. She's dead. Her body is jammed into the rocks out toward the end of the breakwater."

Castle's pale face whitened further.

"Did you call the police?" pursued John.

"Not for now."

"Why not?"

"Privacy," explained Pansy, idly stirring her drink with a straw.

14

Pansy trudged along the hard wet sand toward the Smart's Rock breakwater. She thought she could make out the spot of dark blue among the boulders that marked Mamadou's still-undiscovered body. It was low tide and breezeless. Back the way she had come a tall man walked away from the foot of the seawall ladder. With his long stride he would soon overtake her.

She had seen him during breakfast at Pat and Arthur's. Pat and Arthur's was locally famous for large, succulent breakfasts. She had seen him in person only once before, but going through the police mugbook had fixed his face in her mind: Ali Abdussalam, cross-referenced in police files as Eldee Germaine. He had been sitting at the counter, and Pat had served him corned beef hash with two eggs in the bantering way she served her regular customers. Ali Abdussalam, after all, had lived just across the street for some time before his temporary relocation to New York.

Pansy was squatting by a tidal pool with her arms clutched around her knees when Eldee Germaine caught up with her.

"Look like worm tracks," she said without looking up, "but you can see they're being made by little shellfish who burrow in where the track ends."

"There was three of us—me, Mamadou, and you, wasn't there."

"Now there's only two," said Pansy. She looked up and back over her shoulder. Eldee Germaine looked immense and dangerous glaring down at her.

"Right. Now there only two," he said as Pansy rose and turned to face him.

"What happened to Mamadou?"

"Rocks is slippery."

"She slipped and fell?"

Eldee grinned. "Rock slipped outta my hands."

Pansy looked closely at his hard face. "What's it like to dance in a mystic trance to the Sufi violin? Does it change your whole life?"

"You understand. Arnold Muhammad and Mamadou stole the violin from the man. Try and sell it. The man gotta get it back."

"Is it like floating? Do you think about anything?"

"Never was Mamadou's. She just a thief. Fuckin' around here for. Get in trouble."

"Do you feel the others around you? Do you hear the music, or just feel it?"

Eldee looked down into Pansy's sincere green eyes. "I guess you sorta just feel it. Ain't nothing like it. But I don't dance. Hear that music, I can't even move. Why we gotta get it back, give it back to the man so he can play it."

"How did you become a Sufi?"

"Arnold Muhammad. Dead now. Somebody shot him. Arnold Muhammad and me used to knock off cars 'round Morningside Drive. Later Arnold become a Sufi. But I don't take any that shit. Then he take me to a meeting, this man play the violin. I couldn't even move."

"Changed your whole life, didn't it?"

Eldee started to reply and then stopped himself. The ferocity that had ebbed from his face returned. "Why you doing this shit?" He reached threateningly for Pansy's upper arms, but she slipped inside his grasp and pressed herself against him with her arms around his waist and her cheek on the rough wool of his jacket.

"I'll never be afraid with you to protect me," said Pansy in a warm, endearing voice.

"Protect you? You see Mamadou? I scare away Sidney and Thaddeus just looking at them. Mamadou harder, and Mamadou dead. You don't give up that violin, I'm warning you."

Pansy replied firmly, "You know, Eldee—I like that better than Ali—you're a rotten excuse for a Muslim. If you don't get the violin, you're going to have to answer to the man. Right? Well, I'll tell you something very real, Eldee. If you or anyone else hurts me even a little bit, you won't get jack-shit."

Pansy glided her hand over the smooth skin below John Anderson's navel and marveled at the feel of his steely abdominal muscles. His body was almost hairless.

"I'll answer three questions truthfully if you will," said John softly in the dark. "You can go first."

"All right. But I'm warning you, I read a book that said that lying is involuntarily betrayed by contractions of the scrotum. First. Was your name John Anderson when you were a little boy?"

"Yes."

"Two. Are you yourself a member of the Pahlavaniya?"

"No."

"Okay, here's three. If the violin isn't found, what will happen?"

"The Pahlavaniya will dissolve. Even if Shaykh Zack makes a new one using Castle's copy of the message, his successor will never be able to make it play. There can't be two Sufi fiddles in the world."

"You make it sound like the violin really is miraculous."

"That's a fourth question. It's my turn. And I should warn you I can detect an untrue answer by tone of voice. I read a book about it."

"I am fearless and pure."

"First question: Are you in love with Castle Winter?"

110

"Yes."

"Well, you certainly don't show it."

"I haven't debugged him yet. His program still hangs whenever it gets to a romantic part. He's like a beautiful sleeping prince. I just haven't figured out the right thing to do to wake him up."

"Great. And meanwhile . . . Never mind. Second question: Were you really a high school English teacher?"

"Yes again. I was an undergraduate education major at the University of Wyoming. After getting my credential, I boldly went forth to teach T.S. Eliot and Dylan Thomas to students whose idea of literature was *The New Mutants* and *Classic X-Men*. They could quote me whole Spiderman plots verbatim, and I had a terrible memory for even the best known lines of great poetry. After battling for two years I defected to their side. Now I'm addicted to comic books and computer games. That's where the true creativity of our generation lies."

"What a ghastly thought. Now for three. Where's the violin?"

"I gave it up to fate. I left it on the seat of an uptown A train and got off at 110th Street."

"My dear, one of your answers was a lie," said John in a theatrically sinister voice.

"One of yours was, too, my dear," replied Pansy.

"It's ironic," said Castle, pacing up and down the small living room. "You have these things called controlled substances, which presumably means that other substances should be called uncontrolled substances. But one of the defining characteristics of the controlled substances is that they're uncontrolled. You can find out more easily how much uncontrolled tobacco is produced each year, who buys it, and what it is used for than you can how much marijuana is produced and what becomes of it, but marijuana is a controlled substance."

"My dear, that irony is what enables the DEA to secretly

rule the world," replied John absently from the opposite lawn chair, where he was perusing a *Boston Globe*.

Castle had changed into casual clothes at Anchor Asway and driven back to join them for dinner. John was dressed in an embroidered Japanese lounging robe that exposed huge V-shaped expanses of muscular torso and thigh. Castle could see Pansy's head and shoulders through the window between the living room and the kitchen. Her shoulder motions and the accompanying noises were consonant with doing the dishes. Presently she emerged into the living room. She was wearing a sweatshirt that descended to the top of her thighs and, as far as Castle could see, nothing else. His face crimsoned as he stared at her bare legs.

"Oh, stop it, Castle! I've got underwear on. Let's find somewhere else to eat tonight. I think we've been to Pat and Arthur's once too often."

"I like Pat and Arthur's," said Castle.

Over a fish dinner at The Daily Ketch, Castle filled them in on his progress. He had finally grasped Moe Maghee's inventory control system and wanted to bore them with it.

"You see, everything is shipped in a special DJones container. Depending on how large the order is, shipping boxes are sent to the DJones finder who is buying the substance. Each box has a serial number on it. The box is weighed before it leaves the tower. When the finder packs it, he weighs it full, puts a note recording the weight inside, and seals the box with a lead seal. From that point until it reaches the tower it is never opened. It travels by military mail. When it arrives, the seal is inspected. If it is intact, the box is weighed. The weight is compared with that noted on the slip of paper inside. If a single gram is missing, it means someone is pilfering. But, in fact, they have a perfect record. I suppose because these Pahlavanis are absolutely loyal."

John and Pansy slapped each other's hand away from the last lemon wedge.

"Thank you for your attention. We can get some more lemon," said Castle sarcastically. He flipped to the next page of a little notebook. "You wouldn't believe how many different kinds of controlled substances there are."

"Yes, I would," said John. "It's how I make my living."

Castle studied the notebook. "Now we come to personnel. Donald Jones is a native-born American. Before setting up DJones Chemical Supply Company he worked for a company that sold specialized computer chips. He says he never traveled outside the country until he got into the controlled substance business, but now he goes all over the place. But never to Oman, he says. When I get a chance, I want to see if I can find his passport.

"Then there's Maghee. Jones calls him Moe, so I had this brainstorm that Maghee might be an English spelling for Makki, and Moe might be short for Moses, which is the English form of Moosa. Get it? Moses Maghee: Moosa Makki? Anyway, Jones says Moe is short for 'Slo-Mo' because he does everything so deliberately. Turns out his full name is Francis James Maghee, and the accent is Maine.

"Next. Ali Abdussalam, Pansy's M. Mustafa friend from the police station. Payroll records show he and Moe Maghee have been with the company since it was started. Ali's a driver, general worker, and radio operator. I haven't seen him at the tower yet, but he's still living at Six Sixth Road." Pansy and John wore identical glazed looks. "Hello. Is anybody awake? This is what I'm committing a serious criminal offense by impersonating a government official for."

"Sorry, Castle. I just think it's time for John to tell us something about Moosa Makki before we go any further," said Pansy, staring past the fishnet curtains into the dark parking lot.

John dabbed his lips with his napkin. "And what, pray tell, should I tell you?"

Pansy turned her head and looked at him seriously. "Why don't you know what Moosa Makki looks like?" John put on a hurt pout. "I mean it. Someone's been killed now, and you talk about killing Moosa Makki. Killing gives this whole program a very serious and not very fun tone. But we're still going along with this silly idea that Moosa Makki has a secret identity that has to be uncovered. Bullshit! If good old Shaykh Zack could instruct you to kill somebody and get the damn violin back, he surely could have told you what the bastard looked like. Know what I mean?"

Castle gazed in amazement at his beloved. Where had this resource of logic and practicality lain hidden? What had provoked its being revealed? And then, of course, why *didn't* John know what Moosa Makki looked like?

"Inconsistencies, inconsistencies," said John. "I am afraid, dear Pansy, that you are losing your wonderful capacity to suspend disbelief. But I suppose questions must have answers. Or would you believe that the Arabic dialect of Oman is so marvelously ambiguous and elliptical that the description Shaykh Zack gave me of Moosa Makki could fit absolutely anyone?"

Castle and Pansy shook their heads in unison.

"Okay, then, the truth of the matter. Shaykh Zack was once a sincere mystic. But over time he changed into the vicious, murderous old thug he is today. Yet he is still the genuine grand master of the Pahlavaniya, and its members are absolutely loyal to him. He led the order from traditional smuggling into international drug dealing. They do at least two hundred million dollars a year in business. Until two years ago there wasn't any Pahlavani action in the United States, though. Shaykh Zack thought that wouldn't be smart. Then the DEA got a tip that there was a new network here, and an investigation was begun. You can imagine their surprise when they traced the tip to the Pahlavaniya, and the Pahlavaniya to an old fort in Nizwa. I wasn't surprised, of course, because I already knew the Pahlavanis dealt in drugs in other countries. Naturally, since I was already assigned to Oman to track Green Mountain Blue and knew my way around, DEA assigned the case to me. I got the Sultan, who is actually a dear friend, to appoint me to the guard of the Nizwa fort.

"That, I don't mind telling you, was rather tricky. My makeup and costume were flawless, but my Arabic wasn't.

So I was said to be a mute retainer of the Sultan's father who had served him loyally as a headsman in public executions but was now rather an embarrassment in modern Musqat. The other guards at the fortress, all Pahlavanis, were ordered to let me come and go as I pleased. We hoped that they would assume that I was actually a spy for the Sultan and keep their distance from me, and that, in fact, is what happened. My cover in the date factory, of course, had been long established, so I just had to make sure no one ever saw the old guard entering the factory consultant's house.

"I learned about the violin and Moosa Makki by picking up information around the town. There are lots of Pahlavanis in Nizwa. When you showed up, Castle, I still hadn't made as much headway as I wanted. In particular, I still didn't know anything specific about Moosa Makki except that he was an American who had been passed over for leadership and that two of his disciples disappeared at the same time he did. I guessed that he had started up the network in the U.S."

"What about the shaykh shooting me?"

"I'm sure he intended to leave you in the hole and let you die. If you didn't know where the violin was, you were of no use to him. But you might be a danger to him. He had already gotten from you the copy of the inscription he needed to make a new violin. When I pulled you out of the hole, of course, it became obvious to everyone who had done it. The fortress was closed at the time, and the crazy old executioner from Musqat was the only non-Pahlavani who had access to it. After that, I couldn't safely appear in that disguise any more, and it seemed wisest to leave altogether. From the DEA point of view, the problem was: Assuming Moosa Makki has set up a Pahlavani drug ring in the States, who is he? Where is he? And how can we get the violin back to keep some other Pahlavani from taking over the operation once we bust Makki?"

Pansy and Castle looked at John. John sipped his coffee. Pansy and Castle looked at each other.

"Do you think it's still bullshit, Castle?"

"I don't know. It's sure different from his other story, though."

"Why did you give us all that other crap about going on a mission for Shaykh Zack?"

John squeezed his jowls between his thumb and fingers and pulled the loose, wrinkled skin downward in a gesture of reflection. "Why did I give you all that other crap?" he repeated, as if the question itself was a marvel of philosophical acumen. "Two reasons, I suppose. No, maybe three. But two I'm sure about. The first is that everything Castle said about you, Pansy, told me that you would help a romantic adventurer on a weird and mysterious quest a hell of a lot sooner than you would help a straight arrow DEA investigation. And you're the one who knows where this goddam violin is that I wish I had never heard of."

"I told you. I left it on the A train."

"What!" exclaimed Castle, almost toppling off his chair.

"Oh, forget it, Castle. It's a joke between me and John."

"And the second reason is that Moosa Makki is obviously a clever and unscrupulous man, and he doesn't have the violin either. He wants to find it just as much as I do. It's the key to his control of his network. Thanks to you, Pansy, we can be fairly sure that Makki is connected to DJones Chemical Supply Company, but we still don't have the slightest idea how. Maybe he's Donald Jones. Maybe Jones is a front man. So it's better to have Castle acting as a decoy to smoke Makki out than to just bust into the tower and say the jig is up. We might miss Makki altogether. Now Castle is a good citizen, but after being shot and left to die he, too, may well have been reluctant to participate in a straightforward police operation. But since I knew how he felt about you, Pansy, I knew that if you were involved, he could hardly refuse."

"John," said Castle angrily, his right eyebrow jerking spasmodically, "I deeply resent—and I'm serious about this—I deeply resent being talked about as if I'm a puppet who can be manipulated by sentiment. I also resent being called a decoy when I am actually doing a serious investigation. In fact, as of now, I quit." Nobody said anything. "I mean it."

Pansy put her hand on his. "Let me explain something, Castle. In Shadowgate there's this room you get to in the castle that shows a bunch of drunken ogres in armor lolling around a table." Pansy's voice had suddenly recovered its usual playfulness. "So you wonder, naturally, what's the secret of the room? But no matter what you try to do, the ogres wake up and kill you. The secret of the room, you finally figure out, is that it doesn't have any secret. To win you have to just go on by and forget about it."

Castle felt confused. "What's Shadowgate?"

"A high-res text adventure. The point is, Castle, that we have to just accept the fact that most of what John says is full of it. What counts is the game, and he's just another obstacle."

"But what's the object of the game?"

"To solve the violin mystery. And for that you have to keep on at DJones Company. DJones was entirely my lead, not John's. We should just ignore John." Pansy cocked her head at him.

"I don't get it," said Castle plaintively.

"Let me explain it this way: If you keep on pretending to be a GAO investigator, I'll tell John here he has to sleep on the floor of someone else's apartment."

"I don't get it either," said John.

"We're pretending for a while that Mamadou isn't dead," said Pansy. "Death makes everything too serious."

15

"I have an absolutely fascinating bit of information!" exclaimed Castle as he strode through the door. He took off his overcoat and threw it on a green lawn chair.

"I want you to go sit on the stool in the kitchen, Castle. We're going to do an experiment," replied Pansy. She was sitting cross-legged on the rust orange carpet fiddling with a tiny tape player.

Castle opened his briefcase and pulled out some papers. "You'll never guess what substance DJones is being asked to buy. Where's John? He'll love this."

"I told you I was throwing John out. He's gone. Now go in the kitchen and sit on the stool."

Castle put the papers on the other lawn chair. "Where'd he go? I want him to hear this. What's with the cereal boxes?" Castle had noticed that the rectangular opening between the kitchen and the living room was half blocked by four cereal boxes and one cracker box leaving an opening scarcely a foot wide in the middle.

"Just go in the kitchen and sit, Castle. I think John got himself a room at the Anchor Asway. What we're going to do now is a personality experiment. What kind of music do you like? I've got Tracy Chapman, Dvorak's *New World Symphony,* and The Grateful Dead."

"I don't like any music at all," said Castle, going through the archway into the kitchen.

"All right. I'll choose The Grateful Dead, then." Pansy put a cassette into the tiny tape player, and a strong rhythm sounded thinly from its minute speaker. "Now, lean forward and look through the space in the middle. Good. Now put a quarter on the ledge. Remember, the rules are you have to stay in the kitchen."

Castle put the quarter on the ledge, and Pansy began to dance in place, shifting her weight from one foot to the other and accentuating the swing of her hips. Slowly she unbuttoned her oversized green shirt. "Okay, now I'm taking off my shirt, Castle." She pulled her shirt open and took it off. "Got it? Let me turn around." She sinuously turned so her back was to Castle and then continued around to face him again. "Okay?" She put her hands up behind her back. "Now I'm going to take off my bra." She suited her action to her words, discarding the garment on top of the green shirt on the floor. "So these are my breasts, okay? Let me shake them a little. They're usually described as pert or perky, except for one moron who said they were too small. As if he wanted to be stuck with two cantaloupes on his chest all his life. You can put another quarter on the ledge."

Castle wrenched himself from his gape-mouthed, trans-fixed state and quickly fished a quarter from his pocket. Pansy added a sinuous twisting of her torso to her dance. "Ready for the Levi's, now? . . . Castle?" Castle's face looked like a wax mask with beady black eyes. "Castle, can you hear me? Just blink if you're not ready for the Levi's." She waited. "Okay, then. Here we go." She unbuttoned the waistband of her jeans and unzipped them. Castle strained forward, his head between the boxes. Pulling off her jeans revealed that she was wearing candy-striped bikini under-pants. Pansy danced around in a circle. "Another quarter, Castle?" Castle already had one in his hand. He placed it next to the two others on the ledge. "That was quick." Pansy slipped her underpants down and discarded them on the floor. She danced in place. "Well, there you have it. The epicenter of world history. Primary focus of art, literature, and religion. Same color as the hair on my head. Let me turn around once more. 'Cute little behind' is the usual phrase, but don't let me put words in your mouth," she said over her shoulder. "Forward again. Last look. Look close. Going, going, gone." Pansy picked up her underpants and stepped into them. She danced for a few seconds more and then stepped into her Levi's. "You don't have to pay quarters for this part." She redonned her bra, and finally put her green shirt back on. She abruptly stopped dancing. "You can come out now, jerk."

"What in the world was that all about?" came Castle's bewildered voice from the kitchen, along with the sound of the stool scraping on the floor. He appeared in the archway. "What kind of thing was that for me to come back from work to? I mean, you just don't do something like that without any warning or anything."

"It was an experiment to see whether you really preferred to be simply an impassive voyeur in life or whether you knew how to seize opportunity when it stared you in the face, so to speak. Guess which side won."

"But I didn't know what you were getting at. You told me to stay in the kitchen."

"Right," said Pansy sarcastically.

"Was I supposed to come out and rape you or something?"

"Something! Anything! You just sitting there and paying made me feel like a dancer in a peepshow, and a damned cheap one at that."

"I made you feel like a cheap dancer?" screeched Castle. "You're the one who set it up. I had no idea what was going on. How do you know what a peepshow is like anyway?"

Pansy put her arms around him and hugged him warmly. "Castle, tell me," she said softly. "What's the matter with you? You're healthy. Your body's not bad. You're not old. You have a face like a god. Why are you such a turkey? Were you like this before you got married? For that matter, how did you ever manage to get married?"

Castle's swollen outrage suddenly deflated, and he slumped on the lawn chair holding his papers. "Can you turn that music off? It's very annoying. Music always annoys me." The music stopped with a click. The room suddenly seemed emptier. He looked up at Pansy beseechingly. "You have a beautiful body, Pansy."

"I'll leave it to you in my will. Don't change the subject. Come on, what's with you, Castle? You're buggy. Your program doesn't run." She got on her knees in front of Castle's chair and put her hands on its arms. "I'm good at buggy programs, Castle. I fix them. We had a word processing program that every time you set it to indent paragraphs, it overshot the right margin by one character—but only when you used a laser printer. On page setup it looked perfect. It was a real problem. No one could find the bug. But I was the one who found a work-around for it. So what's your problem? If we can't fix it, maybe we can do a work-around."

"Maybe if we just went to bed together . . ." ventured Castle.

"Castle, that's avoidance. That's like saying that because you can score big in a game like Tetris it doesn't make any difference that the sound doesn't work and the background pictures are full of zigzags. Getting your hands on my cute little behind isn't going to enable you to stop a guy on the street tomorrow and ask him the question that will make you a million dollars."

"But I don't want—"

"Example."

Castle looked away at the three quarters lying between the cereal boxes and then back at Pansy's purple-lipped frown. He tried to conjure up the bounce of her perky breasts.

"It's my teeth," he said at last.

"Your teeth? What's wrong with your teeth? They look fine."

"I know, but they weren't always this way." He opened his mouth and pointed. "You see here? These four upper incisors used to stick almost straight out, and these lower canines, when I closed my jaw, actually came in front of the uppers, which were sort of slanted backward. It looked disgusting."

"Or at least you thought it did."

"I and every kid in all of my classes when I was growing up. I looked like a buck-toothed bulldog. They called me 'Snaggletooth.'"

"And that's why you're a jerk?"

Castle nodded his head sadly. "Yeah, I think so." He nodded again more decisively. "I'm pretty sure it is. I've thought about it a lot, particularly since Judith left me. As an adolescent I always hated to talk or smile, just hated it. And after you've heard that the girls are offering money to whoever dares to kiss you, you don't try very much."

"When was that?"

"Ninth grade."

"Ninth grade? Castle, that must have been thirty years ago. Besides, your teeth look terrific now. And you did get married."

"I know. But I had gotten into these very timid habits."

"How did you ever get married to what's-her-name? Was she ugly, too? Did you wear a sack over your head?"

"Judith."

"Right."

"Judith was my orthodontist's dental hygienist. She had seen worse, she said. But she had great faith in Dr. Machoir. And great faith in me. She was convinced that after Dr. Machoir had finished with me, I would look and act like a romantic movie star."

"Half right, huh?"

"I guess. She kept waiting for me to develop. That's the word she used, as if I were going to go through adolescence again. When I didn't, she gave up and left."

Pansy reached out and squeezed Castle's slack cheeks between her thumb and fingers so he looked like a fish. "Well, I'm not Judith, Castle. I'm going to find a way to make you slay a dragon and carry off a damsel with perky breasts and a cute little behind even if I have to let my hair grow out and switch to red lipstick."

"I like your hair," said Castle meekly.

"Don't talk like a wimp. Tell me now what the piece of

information was that you were so eager to talk about when you came home."

"Oh, that. I had forgotten. DJones has just gotten an army request for three kilos of Green Mountain Blue. The order describes it as 'a substance reputed to be produced either in Libya or Oman and having a strong hallucinogenic effect that can be experienced through contact with the skin.' Contact with the skin! John will love it."

"Sounds like neat stuff."

"Yo, Cecile! It's me, Frankie. Whatcha starin' at? Snap out of it." Frankie's round-faced, bovine sister focused her brown eyes with effort and gave her brother an adoring look. "I thought you'd fainted, or something."

"Frankie, that was the most beautiful music I ever heard."

"Piece of cake," replied her brother, brandishing his bow. The telephone rang. Frankie picked up the receiver.

"Yo, it's me, Frankie . . . Pansy! How ya feelin'?" A pause. "No way! I ain't goin' nowhere for you again." A pause. "They wouldn't let me in there." A pause. "What letter? You gonna send me a letter? They still not gonna let me in." A pause. "Whaddya mean, won't hurt to try? It take me away from the violin. Pansy, get this. How do you get to Carnegie Hall?" A pause. "Nah, practice ain't enough. You need magic, and I got magic. By the way, you and the jerk makin' it up there yet?" A pause. "Ain't my business goin' to no Harvard Club, neither. But I'll do it. Hang in there, Pansy!" He replaced the receiver in its cradle and took up his bow again. "Cecile, you wanna hear me do 'Yesterday'?"

In Marshland, Pansy hung up the phone and fished a manila envelope marked "Violin Quest" out of her suitcase. She looked through the papers until she found the letter Castle had received from a professor at Harvard telling him which African languages the violin message was not in. She looked closely at the letterhead and the signature. Should Xerox OK, she thought.

16

Standing well back in the shadows of the living room to avoid being seen peering out, Pansy watched the black pickup truck with the two black men in it drive for the second time down the far side of the wide main street, past Pat and Arthur's Restaurant, to its end. There a narrow private road continued on toward the seawall, but general traffic made a U-turn around a double row of diagonally parked cars in the middle of the street. The truck U-turned and drove slowly past the front of her apartment. She saw the man with the high flat-top survey the doors marked 1 and 2 on the porch. The March sun not yet having passed the meridian, there was no way he could see into her apartment without getting out and climbing up on the porch.

They don't know whether I'm in 1 or 2, she thought. The pickup proceeded to the opposite end of the double row of cars and U-turned again to the opposite side and into an empty parking space. Now they're thinking about it, she thought. Now they're getting out and talking. Shit! They're going into Pat and Arthur's to think about it some more. Want something done right, have to do it yourself. I sure hope Eldee was telling the truth about them being chickens.

Pansy tore the back flap off the dustjacket of *Korean Foot Massage: A Book That Will Change Your Whole Life*. On the back she scribbled a message in her most harried-looking handwriting. She grabbed a green scarf and tied it on her head, pulling on a blue pea-jacket as she opened her door to knock on the door of the neighboring apartment. After a long pause she heard the clank of a walker approaching and a man's faint, concerned voice saying "I'm coming." The man who opened the door was a slippered and bespectacled octogenarian with thinning gray hair. He wore a maroon cardigan spotted with small burn holes. Pansy felt a rush of warm air redolent with pipe smoke. "Yes?" said the man. "Oh, it's you. You live next door. It's nice to meet you."

"It's nice to meet you, too. I'm Pansy Garden." The old man was about to reply, but Pansy rushed ahead. "Could you do me a big favor?" she said with a beaming smile. "When my boyfriend comes back from work around five-thirty, I'm going to be out. Could you give him this message? He doesn't have a key, and I don't want to leave the message on the door. It's kind of a joke, and if someone else saw it, they might take it the wrong way. I want you to tell him you found the note on the porch."

"*Found* the note?"

"Yes. You can say you heard noises on the porch, and when you looked out, you found the note. I'm playing a little trick on my boyfriend."

"I see. And your boyfriend is the dark, good-looking one or the one with the—"

"Lined face? It's the good-looking one. Things didn't work out with the other one."

"Oh, I'm sorry. I didn't mean to pry. Just wanted to make sure I got the right man."

"No problem. And thank you very much. I'm sorry I have to run now."

The old man extended his hand. "Leander Jackson," he said. "I won't hold you up."

Pansy shook hands. "It's very nice to meet you, Mr. Jackson. Sorry I have to run. Bye-bye."

The old man watched Pansy trip down the porch steps. He shut the door and clanked back to his electric reclining chair. He carefully set the walker aside so the long-handled gripper, with pincers at the end for grabbing things that were too low or too high, was in easy reach. He leaned back against the raised seat of the chair, pressed a button, and amid the whir of an electric motor and the screech of vinyl upholstery rubbing against itself slowly redescended into geriatric comfort. Once again embraced in the chair's most luxurious position, he set a match to a half-filled pipe from the ashtray on his side table, satisfied himself it was properly lit, and unfolded Pansy's note.

Dearest Snaggletooth—

I have been kidnapped by Thaddeus and Sidney Monroe, Mamadou's cousins. They are driving a black Ford pickup license number MXL 762. I know you can't go to the police, but PLEASE RESCUE ME! If I can, I will leave my green scarf to signal where they have taken me.

"Some joke," said Mr. Jackson aloud. "Purple lipstick. I don't know." He put down the note on his side table and picked up the morning's *Marshland Mercury* to resume reading about the drowned body discovered on Smart's Rock.

Across the street, Pansy paused just inside the restaurant door to get control of her fear and then slid into a booth next to one of the two black men drinking coffee. "Are you Thaddeus or Sidney?" she said with a disarming smile.

"Thaddeus," replied the man next to her. "That's Sidney."

"You really do look like brothers." Both men had smooth, youthful faces with high cheekbones and prominent brows. Sidney's head was closely shorn with a line shaved into it on the right side as a part. Thaddeus's haircut was an exaggerated flat-top, short and straight up on the sides, rising to a platform three inches thick on top.

"We've been looking for you," said Thaddeus menacingly.

"I'm in apartment one."

"Estelle says we're supposed to get you.'

"Hey, you got me!" said Pansy jovially. Then she suddenly assumed a sober look. "But do you guys know about Estelle?"

"What about Estelle? She been gone for three days."

Pansy reached over to the next table for the front section of the *Marshland Mercury*. "That article's about her. She's dead."

Sidney turned the paper sideways, and he and his brother read the article together with worried looks on their faces. "How do you know it's her?" asked Sidney. "It says the body didn't have any identification."

"I saw her. I was the one who discovered the body. I telephoned the police anonymously last night."

"There's something not right about this," said Thaddeus. "Estelle didn't have no reason to be in the ocean. She just came up here to find you. And she always had charge cards on her with someone's name on them. She must have been robbed."

"Robbed and murdered, I would say," agreed Pansy.

"You think she was murdered?" said Thaddeus. "What would anyone murder Estelle for? She was just trying to get her violin back."

"Tell that to a big guy named Ali Abdussalam."

"Ohhh . . . you mean Eldee. We seen him. He's a mean mother. He used to be close with Arnold Muhammad, the man Estelle used to live with. Estelle thinks Eldee killed him after Arnold wouldn't give back the violin. Maybe now Eldee thinks Estelle has it. But she don't. You still got it, don't you?"

"I know where it is, and I'm the only one who does. Why don't we go to your place and talk? I don't feel very safe in my apartment now that Estelle's been killed. If you guys can protect me from Eldee, I can cut you in on the violin. What do you say?" Pansy looked apprehensively from one face to the other to determine whether she was going to go with them as their prisoner or their partner.

Five-thirty came and went. At ten Mr. Jackson heard steps on the porch and reached for his walker. The footsteps had stopped but hadn't retreated by the time he made it to the door, so he opened it and turned on the porch light.

"Oh, sorry. Wrong person."

"Quite all right," said John Anderson, who had been standing in the dark dressed in workman's coveralls and a baseball cap. He had a thin strip of metal in one hand and a screwdriver in the other. "My friend has locked me out, but she won't let me take my things. I saw her leave earlier, and she hasn't come back, so I'm taking this opportunity to break in. This porch light helps."

"I see," said Mr. Jackson, peering at a quarter-round molding that Anderson had pried from the doorframe. The old man leaned on his walker, his knees bent and his slippered feet splayed apart. "It's probably illegal, breaking in."

"Well, I should *hope* so," replied Anderson as he insinuated the metal strip into the crack between the molding and the doorframe. "You can't have people just going around and breaking into one another's houses, can you."

Mr. Jackson watched Anderson's futile poking with the metal strip. "Have you had much experience at this?"

"Book learning only, I'm afraid. Or maybe I should say TV learning. I've already completely mutilated my Brooks Brothers card trying to push it into the crack in the door. It dog-legs, you see, before it gets to the latch . . . probably to keep people from breaking in. I thought I could get a better line if I pulled the molding out and then bent this strip and worked it around the dog-leg." He looked at Mr. Jackson, who leaned forward, taking definite interest in the mechanical problem. "You don't know how to pick a lock, do you?"

"Locks are very interesting. I know how they work, but I don't know how to pick one. Have you tried this window next to the door? It's open a crack."

"Since it is, indeed, open, I would feel quite stupid if I hadn't thought of trying it. But I know Pansy nailed it so it couldn't open more than six inches. She didn't want anyone breaking in. So that's why it's hard to break in."

"What about this?" Mr. Jackson had pulled the long gripper from the bag on his walker. "Maybe you can reach the doorknob through the window and use the pincers to turn it."

In less than a minute the door was unlocked. "Thank you, sir," said Anderson.

"Don't mention it," replied Mr. Jackson. He extended his hand. "My name's Leander Jackson. I'm retired."

"John Anderson," replied Anderson, shaking his hand.

"Could you do me a favor, Mr. Anderson?"

"I owe you one."

"Your friend Miss Garden left a note with me for the other gentleman, who was supposed to get here at five-thirty. She said it was a joke. Well, sir, it's after ten now, and I have to start my going-to-bed ritual. Takes about an hour. So maybe if you're going to be here for a while, you could give it to him. He doesn't have a key so she couldn't leave it for him inside, but now that the door's open . . ."

"I'd be delighted."

"You're supposed to tell him you found it on the porch."

"Found it on the porch."

"It's part of the joke."

The two men parted, Mr. Jackson to his going-to-bed, John Anderson to an examination of the strange diagrams contained in Pansy's "Violin Quest" envelope, secure in the knowledge that Pansy would not return until "rescued."

Two hours later John Anderson walked into the Anchor Asway motel. His coveralls had given way to a business suit and overcoat. He was about to ascend the stairs to his room when an unwonted bright spot of color caught his eye in the beige ordinariness of the first floor corridor. A green scarf was tied around the doorknob of a room on the left halfway down.

"Go get 'em, Snaggletooth," said John Anderson with a chuckle. Then he headed up the stairs.

17

Castle Winter was alone in the dark.

He had started out the day in exuberant spirits, his mind resolutely fixed on the equation that slaying a dragon equals perky breasts and a cute little behind. Before going into the DJones submarine tower he had boldly peered through the end window of the trailer parked near it. On a built-in table next to a narrow bed along its left side was a computer like the one in the tower and a formidably bedialed and beswitched two-way radio. A coat hanging on a hook blocked his view of the right wall. The door was locked.

Castle studied the wires that led from the roof of the trailer through a hole drilled in the doorframe of the tower. He felt empowered by the feeling that at last he was making discoveries.

Inside, after a minimal but nevertheless time-consuming exchange of greetings with Moe Maghee, he settled himself behind the other desk and resumed the perusal of shipping records, which had been his preoccupation for the entire week. Copy of a substance request form for X kilos or ounces of substance Y. Then the list of shipping box numbers, places of origin, and five-digit code numbers of finders. Then the weight of each box when it was sent out and its weight on receipt back at the tower, every entry signed by someone in the military post office and personally by Maghee or

Jones. Finally a receipt from the army acknowledging delivery of substance Y in amount X, the weight being equal to the difference between the incoming and outgoing weight of the sealed shipping boxes.

The records were meticulous, whether the amount was 200 grams or 10 kilos. The places of origin ranged all over the world but with a preponderance from South and Southeast Asia. Castle noted telltale locales: Kabul, Afghanistan; Peshawar, Pakistan; Hong Kong; Manila. Yet even though it was obvious that the network DJones was using was the Pahlavaniya, there was nothing to indicate that the company was using its legal imports as a cover for illegal activities. Nor, on earlier reading through the extensive proposal and contract documents from DJones Chemical Supply Company's negotiations with the army, had Castle noticed the slightest irregularity. The only thing suspicious was that there was no indication how a small new company had found out about the army's needs. But it had presented a plan of operation covering the entire world and an inventory control system that had received excellent ratings from the three contract evaluators. And it had offered the army its services at a very modest cost keyed to DJones's willingness to situate their operation in an already existing army facility.

As he had done many times before, Castle pondered the futility, indeed the inanity, of poring over the records at all. He could understand why Donald Jones had welcomed his inspection. He not only had nothing to hide, but he was genuinely proud of his efficient, low-cost system. What Castle couldn't understand was what John Anderson expected of him. If either Donald Jones or Moe Maghee was really the evil Moosa Makki, it wasn't likely that he would leave a passport or high school yearbook lying around that would say so. And the idea that Castle's mere presence might cause such consternation that Moosa Makki would do something that would reveal himself was predicated on the idea that DJones was the center of an illicit drug network rather than a small-scale business taking legal advantage of the Pahlavaniya's worldwide connections.

131

On the other hand, Mamadou was dead. She could, of course, have accidentally slipped on a rock and fallen into the icy Atlantic, her heavy clothes dragging her down, but that still wouldn't account for her lurking around the Smart's Rock submarine tower. Unless she was just following Pansy.

The meandering pathway of Castle's thinking on the matter had, through repeated trials, become a deep rut that always ended at a choice of three marked doors. The sign on the first read NOTHING IS HAPPENING. Whenever he opened it, a listless voice said, "You're acting like an adolescent. Go back to New York. Forget Pansy. Find a job." The sign on the second read SOMETHING FUNNY IS GOING ON. Whenever he opened it, a quizzical voice said, "Damned if I know what, but hang in there." The sign on the third door read DANGER. Whenever he opened it, a hysterical voice said, "You've already been kidnapped and shot, moron. Get the hell out of here." Castle's problem was that he could never actually bring himself to step through any of the doors after he opened them.

"Lunch?" queried Moe Maghee.

Castle looked up from an old substance order for any amount of something called "Yellow Rain (Bee feces?)." It was one of the few orders that DJones had not been able to fill. "You go on, Moe. I'm not hungry yet."

Maghee did not reply. He painstakingly emptied and cleaned his pipe, ordered the items on the top of his desk, opened the center desk drawer and organized that, and finally put on his parka and headed down the stairs. Castle counted his steps and listened for the distant slam of the door. His mind was once again alive with the thought of slaying a dragon and winning a fair princess.

The clue he had been musing about for several days was the second light switch in the office. The switch by the door controlled the overhead light, but there was another switch near the floor, behind Moe Maghee's desk, that apparently did nothing at all since Castle had flipped it up and down several times without any effect. The meaning of the clue had come to him the night before as he had lain in bed in the Anchor Asway thinking about Pansy. It had given him a sudden jolt of excitement that had momentarily driven soft shaven skull bulges and auburn epicenters of world history out of his mind. What if the switch controlled lights in the empty shaft of the tower underneath the office? A submarine lookout tower must have had room in it for supplies, maybe even for ammunition. It only stood to reason that there was a storage area in the shaft of the tower and that access to it could only be from the office since there was no other external doorway or entrance from the stairwell. And if that were the case, then the light switch would have to be in the office, too, since it would make no sense to go down into a dark cellar.

With his deductions from the night before keenly in mind, Castle looked around the room. Suddenly he discerned a faint square impression in the carpet in the corner of the room opposite the door. It flashed through his mind that Pansy had once told him about a text adventure called Zork III where there was an old man in a cavern who, if you asked him the right question, said something that enabled the quester to see a secret doorway. Castle grinned broadly.

The carpet pulled back easily. The trapdoor came up soundlessly when Castle pulled its iron ring. A flick of the light switch on the wall illuminated the depths below. Castle got on his hands and knees and gazed down. The heart of the tower was only about five feet wide since the stairwell took up over half its volume, and was made narrower still by a twenty-inch-deep tier of storage shelves along the side opposite the stairwell, apparently extending all the way to the ground. A steel ladder led downward through a series of eleven-foot-long grates that formed a succession of catwalks from which the storage shelves could easily be reached.

Castle stifled an urge to close the trapdoor, replace the carpet, and wait to ask permission to explore the hidden floors. He reminded himself that he was an investigator from the General Accounting Office and that it was his right to inspect anything he cared to inspect. Feeling more confident, and knowing that Pansy would be proud of him, he descended the ladder to the first catwalk.

The storage shelves were filled with neatly arranged wooden boxes in several sizes with metal reinforcements on their corners and edges. On the lid of each, to the left of a hasp, was stenciled a four-digit number. To the right of the hasp was stenciled a second number, with the words WGT EMPTY directly below it. Castle looked inside several boxes. They were empty. He looked down to see what was on the shelves on the next lower floor and saw more boxes as well as a stack of what looked like books. He looked at his watch. The hour it would take for Moe Maghee to put every spoonful of his customary bowl of soup into his mouth, deliberately savor its flavor and texture, and swallow it, had forty-five minutes to run. Castle let himself down through the hole where the ladder passed through the catwalk and descended to the next level.

The books turned out to be nothing but a stack of smoothly finished wooden boards of varying thickness. They were of approximately the same sizes and shapes as the several types of boxes, but when Castle compared them, he found the boards were consistently a bit smaller.

The next level down appeared to have the same assortment of boxes and boards. Castle compared the box weights with those he had seen listed on countless order forms and satisfied himself that these were, indeed, the boxes DJones used to import substances. He picked one up marked 2.2 KG WGT EMPTY. About five pounds, thought Castle, as he hefted it. He hefted it again. Doesn't feel like five pounds, he thought.

Castle opened the lid of the box and picked up one of the slightly smaller finished boards. The board fit the inside of the box perfectly. Castle pushed it down to the bottom. It looked exactly like the box floor it was covering. He hefted the box. Feels like five pounds now, he thought. He took the board out again and looked more closely at the floor of the box, exploring it with his fingers. There were slight, threadlike ridges in the center. Glue, thought Castle.

He rapidly checked several more boxes, a marvelous thought taking shape in his mind. If a box weighing 2.2 kilos actually only came up to that weight when it had a board weighing one kilogram glued inside it, the Pahlavani finder who received it for a DJones shipment had only to pry out the false floor to gain himself a one kilogram weight allowance for unauthorized substance. The sealed box would come back to DJones, the kilo of illegal substance would be removed, and the stipulated weight of authorized substance would be delivered to the army.

Castle was dumbfounded. He had actually discovered something. DJones Chemical Supply Company actually *was* illegally importing substances, just as John Anderson had suspected. Donald Jones, therefore, wasn't just an enterprising small businessman taking advantage of the Sufi network of the Pahlavaniya. He was a criminal. And Moe Maghee was a criminal. And he himself, Castle Winter, was on a steel catwalk in the heart of the criminals' concrete tower with the evidence in his hands.

Castle's heart began to beat faster. It was then that the lights went out, and his heart beat faster still. Quickly looking up he had seen the square of light coming through the trapdoor suddenly wink out. Then he was alone in the dark.

"My name is Francisco Delacruz. I have this letter from my professor saying the research he wants me to do."

The elderly patrician in charge of the library of the Harvard Club looked over his half-glasses at the diminutive Hispanic youth in black shirt and trousers and white knit tie standing confidently before him. Despite his wholehearted belief in democratization and minority opportunity, his mind involuntarily turned back to his own college days when democratization had meant admitting a select group of students from public high schools. He looked down through his glasses at a letter from Professor Isaac Ephraim on the letterhead of Harvard's Department of Near Eastern Languages and Cultures.

Librarian
Harvard Club
New York City

Dear Sir:
Please grant permission to my student Francisco Delacruz to look
through the class reports concerning alumni from the 1960s and
1970s. Mr. Delacruz is doing a survey for me on the names Harvard alumni give to their children as part of a history I am preparing of the names of Harvard men. As you know, what name a
parent gives a child can change his whole life. I am looking into
the Harvard data to find evidence for this phenomenon.

Sincerely yours,
Isaac Ephraim
Professor of Ethiopic

The librarian sat Frankie at a large library table in a black
and gold captain's chair with a Harvard medallion on the
back and brought him a pile of books bound in crimson, each
one labeled *Harvard College Class of* something. Frankie
opened the first one and began to read summaries of the
careers and personal lives of bankers, doctors, lawyers, professors, and corporate executives. "Mothers sure get divorced a lot," he murmured after half an hour of reading.

18

After a dreadful minute of fear of the dark, Castle adjusted to the loss of light, and he realized that the inside of the tower wasn't as dark as it should be. He looked down at the level below and saw a narrow band of light coming through the tower's one small window. He cautiously groped his way along the catwalk to the steel ladder and descended toward the light. Decades of dirt had rendered the eight-by-six-inch window almost opaque, but there was light enough for Castle to read his watch. It confirmed his suspicion that he had not lost track of time. Moe Maghee could not possibly have finished his bowl of soup and returned to work. This left two possibilities: either Moe's lunch had for some reason been interrupted, or someone else had closed the trapdoor and turned out the lights. In the latter case, the most likely suspect would be Donald Jones himself, even though his schedule had called for him to spend the full day in Boston meeting with the army.

With an effort Castle suppressed an incipient sense of panic and sat down on the catwalk to think. If he was going to go up and bang on the trapdoor, he had best do it right away. His story would be that he was simply carrying out his commission to investigate all the operations of DJones Company. He could rant in a righteous rage at whoever was there and stomp out. But then what? Was Donald Jones likely ever to let him down into the tower again? If Castle went to the police, could he expect the boxes and boards to be there when the police returned with a search warrant? For that matter, would the police believe him? Would anything he did help him find out who Moosa Makki was or what the message in the violin said? Most important of all, would Pansy consider him brave and resourceful if he took the most obvious way out? Or would she call him names?

Then, on the other hand, maybe his blustering about being a GAO investigator wouldn't work. What was the likelihood that the person who had closed the trapdoor and turned out the lights had already guessed that Castle was poking his nose into illegal business? Since the trapdoor had been up and the lights on, it must have been obvious that someone was downstairs—but whoever had entered the room at the top of the ladder hadn't even called down to him. He had just shut the trapdoor. Why would someone have deliberately shut the trapdoor on him? To keep him from going anywhere, obviously. Castle mused that it wasn't called a trapdoor for nothing.

So someone is keeping me here for some reason, thought Castle. But they're obviously not going to leave me here to starve or die of thirst because they must know that someone will come looking for me. Therefore, they probably intend to keep me here until some particular time for some particular reason.

Castle thought hard and tabulated the possibilities that came to mind. Number one, I have been caught snooping, and they have summoned Moosa Makki to decide what to do with me. In that case, I'll finally find out who Moosa Makki is . . . before he kills me. Number two, they intend to give me a good scare. After a while they'll let me out, make a spurious apology, and suggest that I not come back. Then later they'll kill me to keep me from talking. Number three, they intend to wait until dark and then kill me.

Castle felt a lump of fear in his throat. He looked at his watch again: 2:12. It would be dark in about five hours. The seawall was only seventy feet away, beyond it lay the beach, the Smart's Rock breakwater, and the cold gray Atlantic that had already claimed one life. Castle began to think feverishly. Write a note. Break the window and throw the note out. Find something to write on. Find something to break the window with. Find something to write with. He patted all of his pockets and came up with a ballpoint pen but no paper. How to get someone to pick up the note and read it? Write it on money! Great idea! Castle held his wallet up to the shaft of light from the window. His largest bill was a twenty.

Using a 2.2-kilo shipping box as a lap desk he carefully printed in block capitals on the white margin of bill: MY NAME IS CASTLE WINTER. I AM BEING HELD PRISONER IN THE SUBMARINE TOWER. CONTACT PANSY GARDEN AT 5 SIXTH ROAD APT. 1. TELL HER TO RESCUE ME. YOU CAN KEEP THE MONEY. I'll float it on the wind, thought Castle. Maybe it will carry over to Fifth Road or Sixth Road. He went to the window. The small pane was set six inches deep in the concrete wall. A hit with his fist produced a dull solid sound. Thick, he thought. He wet a bit of his handkerchief with spittle and rubbed at the grime on the pane. When a spot of transparency appeared, he craned his neck and looked down.

"Oh God," he said aloud. A tall bearded black man wearing a white skullcap and green army jacket was standing between the trailer and a blue van with some writing on the side. He was having an animated conversation with a man dressed in coveralls whose face was screened by a black baseball cap. Castle looked for indications of the wind direction and was gratified to discover what appeared to be the string of a tree-wrecked kite trailing from a naked limb. The wind was blowing toward Fifth Road, and the men were closer to Sixth Road. With luck, they would never see the twenty floating to the ground.

Castle searched his pockets and then looked around for something to break the thick window with. He tried several boxes, but they were too big for the opening in the concrete. The smallest box insert slid neatly into the space, but banging it against the thick glass had no effect. Castle made a second groping search along the shelves but came up empty.

No need to panic, he thought anxiously. There has to be something in here I can break the glass with. He looked up into the pitch black. He couldn't remember seeing anything useful on the upper levels. Then he looked down. There seemed to be a slightly lighter patch in the darkness below. Castle descended the steel ladder. After two more levels it ended. He felt the floor in the dark. It was concrete. He looked in the direction of the light patch he had seen from above, but he could see nothing. Holding his arms out he slid his feet forward blindly. After four slides he touched a smooth metal surface. He explored it with his hands and discovered a lever. He pulled the lever. It opened the door of a white refrigerator. The light inside shone forth like a beacon welcoming a frightened sailor home from a storm-wracked sea.

"Ha-hah!" barked Castle triumphantly. "Light wins over darkness again." He looked inside the refrigerator. Several different sizes and shapes of bottles were neatly arranged on the shelves. "Substances," he said in wonderment. He turned four of them to look at their plain white labels. All they had on them were numbers, but Castle recognized the pattern of the numbers as being order number, finder number, and box number. Yet there was nothing in the refrigerator to break the window with, and the door handle seemed firmly attached.

Castle looked around in the wedge of light spilling out of the refrigerator. The ground floor was much larger than the ones above and differently arranged. Storage shelves lined two walls, and the refrigerator was against a third, but the sizes and shapes of the boxes and sacks on the shelves and the floor were unfamiliar. There were only a few of the numbered wooden shipping boxes. Castle drew over a shipping box and put it in the refrigerator door to hold it open. Then he untied the string around the neck of a lumpy cloth sack almost at his feet. Inside were a number of roughly rectangular white blocks of assorted sizes. Castle took one out and held it in the light from the door.

This, he thought, is cocaine . . . or chalk . . . or salt . . . or meerschaum . . . or God knows what. All I need is to risk my neck to escape with one of these, take it to the police as evidence, and have some pompous Egyptian chemist tell me I've liberated a big piece of chalk. He started to smell it and stopped. I don't know what cocaine smells like, he thought. Besides, getting it in my nose will make me high. That wouldn't be smart at all. He started to put the block back in the sack and then thought of what Pansy would say. He pondered. He held his breath, brought the block to his mouth, and licked its long side before drawing it quickly away and dropping it back in the sack.

"Echhh, aspirin," he said as intense bitterness overcame his sense of taste. Moments later his tongue went numb. "Ooops. I guess it is cocaine. Local anesthetic." He had a hard time saying the words. He stuck his tongue out and felt it with his fingers. It seemed to be normal even though its numbness conveyed the impression to the rest of his mouth that it was thick and puffy. "Lucky thing I didn't sniff it."

Castle began looking around the ground floor room. After two or three minutes he became aware of a pounding in his heart. He felt as if he were alert to defend himself, even though there was nothing around to threaten him. As more minutes passed, he felt more and more alert. In fact, he felt more alert and responsive than he had ever felt in his life. Moreover, the back of his head and neck seemed to be floating in the most wonderful way.

He shot his eyes sharply around the room, penetrating every nook and cranny with his acute gaze. He became aware of a musty smell laced with unidentifiable chemical odors that he had failed to notice earlier. Suddenly he looked back at the refrigerator. "That's a refrigerator," he said aloud. He laughed loudly and noticed an echo from on high that he had been unaware of previously. He measured the dimensions of the refrigerator with his sharpened eye

141

and looked back at the hole in the first level catwalk through which the steel ladder descended to the floor.

"This refrigerator didn't come down that ladder," he said triumphantly. He felt as if he were addressing an attentive and appreciative audience. "That means there's another door down here. Furthermore, this room is wide. So the stairwell stops on the level above. That means this must be a basement." His keen, decisive mind considered the evidence. "Stands to reason. You don't build a defensive position without an escape hatch. Suppose a U-boat had landed saboteurs to take out the tower? With only one door, the soldiers would have been trapped." His heart was firmly and confidently pumping energy throughout his body. He surveyed the room once again and in the dark part, shielded from light by the open refrigerator door, spied a semicircular handle set flush to the wall. "Well, what do you know? So in Pansy's Zork III there's an old man who guides you to a hidden door only if you've eaten the right stuff beforehand. Watch out, Pansy, here comes the dragon-slayer."

The semicircular ring flipped out from the wall and turned easily. The heavy door yielded to a gentle push. A passageway filled with inky blackness lay beyond. Castle put his hand to the most likely spot on the left-hand wall inside the passageway and found a double light switch. The first switch lit up the passageway, which after a few feet angled to the left. The second switch lit the lights in the tower behind him. Castle felt gloriously triumphant.

After a minute's deliberation Castle decided that the passageway was leading to the northwest, the direction of Sixth Road. Number 6 Sixth Road, he thought. That was where the man that Pansy traced was living. Obviously, it was connected with the submarine tower underground. What a superb setup for a drug operation. Who would ever associate a little brick bungalow on a dead-end street with the submarine tower? Despite his exhilaration, Castle walked cautiously down the passageway as if expecting it to drop off into empty space. Instead he came to a door at its far end. He turned the semicircular handle and pushed forward.

The bearded black man in the white skullcap he had seen outside the tower was seated next to a tall metal cabinet in a straight chair that leaned against the wall on its back legs. He had a baseball bat across his lap.

"Get on back in there, boy," he said ominously.

Castle's entire body was tensed and exploding with energy. He stepped through the doorway. The man stood up. "You're Ali something or other, aren't you?" said Castle as his eyes darted about for a means of escape.

"Ali Abdussalam. You gonna get back in there, or do I have to hit you one?"

Castle dove forward, jigging to the right to get around his enemy. The baseball bat crunched hard into the upper part of his left arm, which immediately stopped responding to signals from his brain. He fell to the floor and crashed against the wall. Ali pulled him up with one hand while brandishing the bat with the other.

"You dumber than bricks, boy. Now get back in there 'fore I do the same thing to your head." He roughly pushed Castle back through the door and slammed it shut. Castle put his ear to the door and heard him pull his chair closer. Then Castle looked in his right hand. He was holding a piece of brick that had been lying on the floor where he had fallen. Despite the pain and numbness of his left arm, Castle smiled with satisfaction.

With the lights on in the tower, he easily scrambled back to the third level and applied his eye to the clean spot on the window. No one was in sight. The blue van had disappeared. The telltale kite string was still indicating a northerly breeze. Castle gripped the brickbat in his right hand, being careful to keep his fingertips away from the protruding corner. He smashed the brick into the window. A small slab of glass in the center fell out into space, leaving several other pieces still stuck in the frame. Castle took the twenty dollar bill from his wallet and fed it through the hole. When he felt the wind hit it, he let go and saw it immediately shoot upward out of sight.

Satisfied that he had done a remarkably good job of engineering his rescue, he climbed back down the ladder. He identified some sacks of marijuana and arranged them as a cushion on the concrete floor. Then he sat down to wait. Some time later his feeling of exhilaration suddenly waned and he began to feel simply awful.

19

Pansy stretched and yawned and looked over at the two pairs of bare feet next to her folded blanket on the floor. Sidney and Thaddeus were sitting in their trousers on the edge of one of the beds watching the "Today" show.

"Sorry about last night, fellas," said Pansy sleepily. "You're both very nice guys and all. In fact, you're just my type. But I have this thing about men who smell like butter. It just turns me off. You know what I mean? The way to get rid of it is to stick to brown rice, lentils, and lots of carrots for about two weeks." Pansy stood up and shuffled to the bathroom.

"You still got a cute little behind, Pansy," said Sidney good-naturedly as he eyed her panty-clad rump.

"So do you, Sidney," replied Pansy, closing the door.

"What're we gonna do?" said Thaddeus when she came out buttoning her Levi's.

"Well, I've been thinking about that. The fact of the matter is, some other people I know have let me down. So you guys are going to have to be my main men."

"Doing what?" said Thaddeus skeptically.

Pansy sat at the mirror and stabbed at her hair with Thaddeus's Afro rake. "What's our main objective? Money. Right? Arnold Muhammad and Estelle Marie stole the violin because they heard someone would pay one hundred thousand dollars for it, didn't they? Well, they were being fed a line.

The organization takes in over two hundred million a year, and the head man can't keep all the strings in his hands without the violin. It's sort of a cult thing. The violin makes him the boss."

"Cult, huh," ventured Sidney. He turned off the television. "Guys like that can be mean. How much you figure this head man will go for the violin?"

Pansy played with her hair some more and painted her pink lips purple before replying. "Half a million. Two hundred and fifty thou for you; two hundred and fifty thou for me. Only you guys have to make sure I don't get killed like Estelle Marie did."

"And you think she was killed by Eldee?"

"You bet. He virtually told me so. Eldee's the head man's enforcer. Get Eldee out of the way, and then we make a deal with the head man."

"So who's the head man?" asked Sidney.

"The president of the United States. Biggest cult in the country."

Thaddeus and Sidney looked stunned. "You shitting us?" asked Thaddeus suspiciously.

"What do you think?" replied Pansy sarcastically. "You ever hear of the president playing the violin? The truth is, as much as I trust you guys and think you're so cute and all, me knowing who to deal with and how to do it and you not is the best way I know of to keep you from thinking bad thoughts. I get the violin back and do it my way, you get to split two hundred and fifty thou. You cut me out and do it by yourself, maybe through whoever Estelle Marie knew, if you even know who that was, you're likely to get only the hundred thou."

"Uh-uh," said Thaddeus, "you're not a very trusting little girl, are you?"

Sidney cut in. "Pansy, this still don't make a lot of sense. You've got the violin, right? The man wants it back so he can run his cult and make money, right? Then what's Eldee got to do with it? If this cult man's ready to buy the violin back, he don't want to scare away the person who's got it. Right?"

"Absolutely," said Pansy. "Couldn't be righter. But think it out. How did Estelle Marie get the violin?"

"Arnold stole it. He was a friend of Eldee's. Arnold and Eldee belonged to the same Muslim outfit. Then Eldee dropped out, and he and Arnold got in a fight about it. Arnold told Eldee he was breaking the rules. Eldee told Arnold he was stupid. Eldee told Arnold about a guy playing the violin and making everybody nod out like they were stoned. So when Arnold heard about a reward for this violin, he knew right where it was. He come up here and stole it. Estelle was with him."

"They stole it from the tower?"

"'Course. That's where it was. Reason Estelle and us come back up here is she figured you might be trying to make a deal. And here you are, trying to make a deal."

"Did she say who had the violin up here?"

"Sure. Moosa Makki. The guy who runs the place."

"Black guy?"

"No, white guy. American. Picking this funny name is part of his being a Muslim. How come you don't know all this, Pansy, if you say you know who to deal with for half a million?"

"Because the head of the cult isn't Moosa Makki. It's a guy outside the United States. Moosa Makki stole the violin from him, and he wants it back. But Makki wants it back, too. Eldee works for Makki. It's the other guy who will pay the half million."

"Oh, I get it," said Sidney. "This guy outside the country wants to buy the violin back, but Moosa can't do it that way because then someone just steals it again. He's gotta show you can't fuck with him. So that's why you want us to take care of Eldee. Show him you've got some muscle, too. Makes sense."

"Makes a lot of sense, Sidney. Besides, you and Thaddeus don't want Eldee to get away with killing Estelle Marie, do you? Why don't you go on over to Six Sixth Road and see what's up. That's Eldee's place. Call me back here and tell me what's happening."

Sidney and Thaddeus obediently put on the rest of their clothes. "Why don't we all go for breakfast first?" suggested Thaddeus as he pulled on his heavy jacket. "I'd hate to run into Eldee on an empty stomach."

Pansy shooed them out the door with her hands. "How can I eat breakfast when someone wants to kill me? Come on, get going. Give me a call."

Thaddeus untied Pansy's green scarf from the outside doorknob and handed it to her. "This yours, ain't it? You must've dropped it, and somebody tied it on the door." He shut the door behind him.

Fat lot of good that did me, thought Pansy as she tossed the scarf on the bed. Maybe Castle just looks like a prince but is actually an enchanted frog with a frog's emotions, a frog's brains, a frog's sense of romance, a frog's understanding of women . . .

Suddenly the door to the room flew open and slammed against the wall. A policeman with a gun was silhouetted against the light in the hallway.

"Freeze, suckers!" he screamed. "One move, and I'll blow your right hand off so you can never make love again!"

Pansy jumped back and then looked more closely. "John! Where the hell did you come from?"

"Just walk past me out the door, Pansy, and your ordeal will be over."

"Forget it. They're gone."

John Anderson shut the door behind him and replaced the gun in the holster hanging from his belt. "Well, my dear, I already know that. I saw them go. But wasn't it wonderful they didn't leave earlier? I just got back from the costume rental. Isn't this the funkiest uniform you've ever seen? Can you believe this 'Ace Security' on my shoulder? I mean, who in his right mind would hire a security company with such a wildly original name? By the way, you haven't commented on the line after the 'Freeze, suckers.' I thought it was cute."

"John, where's Castle?" said Pansy with exasperation in her voice. "*He* was supposed to rescue me."

"You mean Old Snaggletooth? 'Snags,' as we used to call him when we were sitting around the campfire in Oman. Ah, the good old days. I'll tell you where Castle is after you tell me where Sidney and Thaddeus have gone. I don't want them coming in and surprising me."

"They won't. I sent them off to cause trouble for Eldee. They're supposed to call me here. Anyway, they're perfectly harmless."

"Splendid. Maybe they can bring Castle back from Eldee's. He's being held prisoner."

Pansy held her hand to her mouth. "Oh, John. What are we going to do? Are you sure? That must be why he didn't rescue me. Here I thought he was just being a wimp again. I was even afraid he had gone to the police and gotten us all in trouble."

John held out a piece of paper to her. "Well, you can stop worrying. Here's your note. When he didn't come back to the apartment, Mr. Jackson gave it to me to give to him. Naturally I got worried about the dear, sweet boy—if-anything-should-happen-to-him-may-it-be-on-my-head—and went out looking."

"At night? Like looking for a dog? What did you think he was, lost?"

"You insult my intelligence. I'll have you know, Miss Grapelips, that I haven't been entirely idle during the past two weeks. I am, after all, an agent of the most widely feared drug-busting agency ever paid for by taxes. Three days ago I went to Radio Shack and bought three very inexpensive intercoms and three little voice-activated tape recorders. Then I artfully disguised myself as a gas company man and rented a little blue van and painted a sign on it. Then I went to Six Sixth Road and broke in. I put the little intercoms near windows and ran their little wires outside and put the other end, along with a tape recorder, in a box. On each box I had painted 'Danger—Gas Detector—Do Not Tamper With or Move.'

"Next—I know you must be waiting to find out what I did next—well, next I waited around until I saw Eldee and went up and told him that there was a dangerous gas leak in the piping somewhere in the neighborhood and that because it was an emergency I had had to go into his house, and other people's houses, and place detectors so we could find it before the whole neighborhood blew up."

"And he believed you?"

"At least for the time being. I had a wonderful-looking identification card hanging on my coveralls in one of those clear plastic thingies with a clip."

"All right. So he believed you. I can buy that. Fooling Eldee isn't any harder than hypnotizing a chicken. I can do that, you know. I learned how back on the ranch in Wyoming when I was growing up."

"My dear, I never said you weren't a woman of many cute and perky parts. But you mustn't let your attention stray from your beloved Castle's plight. I assume he's still beloved?"

"Quite beloved," confirmed Pansy. "In fact, my hero. So go on about my hero."

John Anderson produced two tape recorders from inside his blue uniform jacket. "The first one is from the basement." He clicked it on. First there was the noise of something scraping on the floor. Then an artificially high tenor voice came on singing "My Girl."

"Eldee's got a nice voice," said Pansy, "but this audio sucks. It doesn't have any bass."

John Anderson fast-forwarded the tape for a moment. When he started it again they heard Eldee's voice saying, "Get on back in there, boy." Then Castle's voice: "You're Ali something or other, aren't you?"

"That sounds very bold," said Pansy appreciatively.

"Ali Abdussalam. You gonna get back in there, or do I have to hit you one?" Suddenly there was a flurry of bangs and crashes. Pansy put the knuckle of her index finger to her mouth. "You dumber than bricks, boy. Now get back in there before I do the same thing to your head." John turned off the recorder.

"Oh, Castle! At least he's still alive. Can you imagine him

attacking someone as dangerous as Eldee? I mean, that's just incredible! Castle with guts. I simply can't believe it."

"Frankly, neither can I," said John. "Now listen to this one. It's from the kitchen near the telephone." He turned on the second recorder.

First there were the tiny sounds of the buttons on a telephone being pushed. "Moosa?"—it was Eldee's voice—"Eldee. White shit tried to come outta the tunnel. I scared him back in. When you getting back, tonight or tomorrow? Uh-huh. We do him then. Later." John switched off the recorder.

"Anything else?"

"Well, my dear, what more could you want? I mean, really. Your callow boyfriend has suffered injury bravely trying to escape the clutches of a murderous thug and is being held prisoner in a tower. A mysterious evil mastermind is scheduled to show up at any minute and put him in mortal peril. Your two comrades are off scouting the premises. And an intrepid white knight in a pathetically tacky rented uniform is at your side ready to perform the rescue, uncover the identity of the mastermind, and win your heart away from the callow boyfriend. Where are you going to find a text adventure as real as this?"

As if on cue, the telephone rang.

"Pansy," said Thaddeus, "we been watching Eldee, but he just been sitting in his basement with a baseball bat. Then just now a white guy drove up and stormed in there. About six foot, sort of orange hair, real bushy eyebrows. He's down talking to Eldee like he's real angry about something."

"That's Donald Jones," said Pansy into the receiver.

"That's Moosa Makki," whispered John in her ear.

"Stay where you are, Thaddeus, and we'll come right over. Where are you?"

"We're in the pickup. We're parked on Sixth Road between the house and the tower. Who you coming with?"

"A friend of mine named John. You don't know him.

He's in a cop uniform, and he's got a gun, but don't worry about it."

"That's cool. One more thing. Sidney went around side the house and found some funny looking boxes said gas company on them. One had a tape recorder inside it. I'll tell you, somebody else got his eye on this house."

20

Castle woke up stiff and cold. A gray shaft of light angled from the little window twenty feet above him onto the opposite wall. He reached out as he had done half a dozen times during the night and opened the refrigerator door. By the light from inside he saw that it was a little after eight o'clock. At least for the last four hours his sleep had been solid. He got up and flipped the switch in the passageway turning on the lights in the tower. Then he urinated in the shipping box he had chosen as a toilet and closed the lid. He sat down again. There was nothing to do but wait.

He checked his watch at a quarter to ten when he heard the door open at the far end of the passageway. All during the previous afternoon and evening he had contemplated ways of overpowering Ali Abdussalam and escaping but rejected each one. Hitting the big man with a box and then darting past him was patently suicidal. Ali had had a baseball bat—at least—the day before, and there was no telling what he would be armed with this time. The room was small, the passageway was narrow. Ali could swing with his eyes shut and keep anyone from getting past him. Jumping on him from the catwalk or ladder? Equally foolish. Escape up the ladder? He had checked. The trapdoor was bolted. Set a fire? Good way to die happy asphyxiated by marijuana smoke. Besides, no matches. Hide in the refrigerator . . .

and suffocate. The idea of throwing chemicals from the bottles in the refrigerator in Ali's face to blind him appealed to Castle briefly, but he didn't know which, if any, might be corrosive or toxic, and after his accidental high from licking cocaine he was afraid to find out. The last thing he needed was to be zonked on some mind-altering substance and miss the opportunity to escape that might present itself later on.

Footsteps drew closer in the passageway.

"You seem mighty peaceful," said Ali Abdussalam as he entered the basement room, bat in hand. "Did you sleep well?"

"Not bad. My left arm still hurts, though. You didn't have to hit so hard." Castle was amazed at the coolness of his own voice, so completely out of synch with the anxiety he felt inside. "What are we going to do now?"

"Go upstairs see the man."

"Moosa Makki?"

"Right. Go upstairs see Moosa."

"Then what?"

"Then Moosa decide. Go on. Get on up the ladder."

Castle remembered movies in which a hero climbing a ladder had managed to kick down on the bad guy behind him and escape, but he had practiced it the evening before several different ways, and he couldn't figure out how it could work. Jumping or falling, yes, but kicking downward didn't seem physically possible. As he slowly climbed the ladder from level to level the various escape scenarios came back to him, but he kept on climbing. When they reached the top, Ali poked the bat up past him and banged three times on the trapdoor.

The trapdoor opened, and Castle saw the grim face of Donald Jones looking down at him, his wild bushy eyebrows giving him a ferocious look.

"Come on up, Mr. Winter. It's time we had a talk." Donald Jones's hard eyes conveyed the same ominous message as the gun in his hand. Castle docilely climbed out of the shaft and into the office. "Go on ahead of me up the stairs. I think

154

the roof is a suitable place to talk. Ali, you stay down here and make sure we're not disturbed."

Sidney ran up to the van as soon as John and Pansy pulled up outside the brick bungalow. "Something's happening. The guy with the orange hair's gone over to the tower, and Eldee went through a door in the basement. When he didn't come out, we snuck in. There's a passageway down there leading toward the tower. Thaddeus is checking it out."

"You go with Thaddeus," ordered John. "We'll go to the tower."

Sidney looked uncertain.

"It's okay, Sidney," said Pansy. "He's not really a cop."

John and Pansy got out while Sidney ran back into the house to join his brother. "We better leave the van here," said John. "Don't want anyone to see it from the tower."

Pansy followed John down and across Sixth Road. They slipped through the gap between the chain-link fence and the neighbor's picket fence. They were approaching the tower from the side, out of sight from its windows. At the door John produced a ring of keys.

"Where'd you get those?"

"Swiped them from Eldee's kitchen table." The fifth key he tried fit the lock.

"They're going to hear us coming up," whispered Pansy as they crept up the stairs. "This stairwell makes all the sounds go up."

"Not if we're quiet as mice," John whispered back.

"I hear you creeping up them stairs," came a booming voice from above. "You better stop right now 'cause I got a shotgun, and you trespassing on private property."

"That's Eldee," whispered Pansy. She and John continued to creep upward until they came to the last landing.

"Eight steps away," whispered John.

"You could just peek around the corner and shoot him," replied Pansy.

"It's not a real gun. Plastic. Looks just like the real thing if you take the little red plug out of the barrel."

"Oh."

"You all don't come no farther, now," came Eldee's voice.

"We're officers from the Treasury Department, Mr. Abdussalam," shouted Pansy. "Slide your gun down the stairs and then walk down with your hands up."

Eldee laughed. "You Pansy Garden. You ain't no Treasury officer. You just a little girl on the beach."

"Rats," said Pansy under her breath. She shouted again. "Where's my boyfriend?"

"Boy with the pretty face?"

"That's the one."

"He's up on the roof with Mr. Jones lookin' down. They havin' a talk about flyin'."

"Oh God," said Pansy, "he's going to throw him off. John, do something."

"My dear girl, I'm thinking as hard as I can. Thaddeus and Sidney mentioned a baseball bat, not a shotgun. Maybe he's bluffing, and I can just rush him."

Just then came a loud crash from the top of the stairs followed by bumps and scraping sounds.

"Come on up," called Thaddeus. "Eldee's out of the way."

Pansy and John scrambled up the remaining steps to find the figure of Eldee Germaine lying on his back beside the door. Sidney was holding Eldee's baseball bat in one hand and a hammer with blood on it in the other.

"We came up through the trapdoor," said Thaddeus. "He was so busy with you guys he didn't hear us."

"Is he dead?" asked Pansy.

"Nah. Probably got a concussion maybe. Sidney knows how to hit people."

"I'm sure he does," said John.

"No one asked you, cop."

"He's not a cop, Thaddeus," said Pansy. "I told you. He's a friend. He rented the uniform to make it easier to rescue Castle."

"Castle your boyfriend? The one you say's a jerk?"

Pansy was peering up the stairs to the next floor. "Eldee said he's up on the roof with the guy we've been looking for. I think you and Sidney better stay down here with Eldee and let me and John go up. But be ready if we call you." She silently began to creep up the stairs.

"You'll never get away with this, Jones!" Castle shouted to be heard over the noise of the cold sea wind rattling the plastic windscreens. "What you've got in that tower will put you in the penitentiary for twenty years. Your best bet is to turn state's evidence and give us the names of all your agents. I can't guarantee you'll go free, but I'll do what I can."

"Very funny, Winter, considering we're all alone and I've got a gun. I'm sure you did find things in the tower that violate our various substance control acts, but unfortunately that information will die with you when you accidentally fall off this roof."

Though frightened beyond imagining, Castle couldn't keep from thinking about lines from TV crime shows. "I wouldn't try it, Jones. Or should I call you Moosa Makki? I've been in contact with my backup by radio ever since I went into the tower. This place is surrounded. There are four sharpshooters with their sights on you at this very second."

"Four?" queried Jones sarcastically, his orange hair flying maniacally in the wind. "You think that's enough? Why not six? Or fifteen? All hidden, naturally."

"You don't believe me, do you?"

"Of course not. If you had had a radio, we would have picked up your transmission on our radio in the trailer. Besides, I found this caught on one of the windscreens when I was preparing things for your fall this morning." He handed Castle the twenty dollar bill with his rescue message on it. "Pretty ineffective backup device for a man with a radio and a team of sharpshooters on call."

"Pansy Garden is the code name for my backup unit," said Castle defiantly. He stared down at the bill in his hands and was suddenly overcome by a feeling of crushing despair. What a foolish gesture it now seemed. What a silly, senseless quest for nothing at all except getting into bed with a strange and exciting girl. He felt overcome by the cold, the roar of the wind, and a feeling of immense fatigue. He realized that he was going to die and that he didn't want to. But there was nothing more to do about it.

"In case you're interested," said Jones, holding on to a section of the black plastic windscreen, "I've frayed the nylon rope that holds this panel. One push and it'll go. It will look like an accident, so your survivors can probably sue me for negligence. If it makes you feel any better, I'll be willing to settle very generously out of court. It's sort of like an added insurance policy. Much better for everyone than shooting you."

Pansy and John reached the top of the stairs in time to hear the words "insurance policy." The door to the roof was standing open, and the wind was blowing down the stairs. Crouched near the floor, John peered around the corner of the doorframe and then pulled his head back.

"He's got a gun," he whispered, "and he's facing this way. We don't have a chance unless he turns around."

Pansy peeked around the corner and confirmed Anderson's assessment. Castle looked terrified. She took a deep breath and then stood up and strode out on the roof.

"Drop the gun, Mr. Jones! You're under arrest! Pansy Garden. Treasury Department."

Donald Jones looked at her quizzically, and then with malicious amusement, his gun remaining leveled at Castle's chest. "I didn't know the Treasury Department went in for such interesting hairstyles. And I didn't know they sent agents to make arrests without arming them."

"Don't deceive yourself, Mr. Jones. Our studies show that in sixty-three-point-two percent of shootings at point-blank range the projectile either misses the target or fails to stop it. Moreover, in thirteen percent of arms-length encounters between armed officers and suspected perpetrators the perpetrator successfully seizes the officer's gun or causes the officer to shoot himself. Consequently we have adopted an arrest protocol that puts the emphasis on physically subduing the suspect and keeping lethal weapons at a distance."

"That's amazing," said Jones with a chuckle, "just amazing."

"I'm glad you're so amused, Mr. Jones. Our studies also indicate that mental distraction is a key aspect in over three-quarters of successful attempts to physically subdue suspects. To further distract you mentally I might add that Eldee Germaine has been taken into custody. Moreover, this building is surrounded. There are four sharpshooters with their sights on you at this very second."

Jones looked puzzled. "You're sure it's four?"

"Standard arrest protocol. Three's not enough, and five's too many. If you'll just glance out at the seawall, I'll signal for them to show themselves."

Jones started to glance away and then stopped. "Winter, move over into that corner." He gestured toward the northwest corner of the roof under the radio antennas. "Garden, come over here." He paused. "No, don't come over here. Go over with him and make your signal." Jones trained his gun on Pansy and Castle and turned his head so he could see both them and the seawall.

"UP NOW!" screamed Pansy in her loudest voice.

John Anderson exploded from the open doorway behind Jones's back and hurtled across the ten-foot distance separating them. Jones's head and gun moved together toward the sound but not fast enough. Anderson's lowered shoulder smashed into Jones's left side. Jones tipped onto his right leg and windmilled with his arms, trying to get his balance. A look of utter astonishment transformed his features. John put his hands together and gave the tottering man a firm additional shove. The rope holding the windscreen gave way with a loud snap. Pansy and Castle caught a momentary glimpse of Jones's face, his astonishment given way to horror, before he disappeared from sight. The thump as he hit the ground was barely audible over the cold wind's roar.

21

"You didn't have to kill him."

"I most certainly did."

"No, you didn't. You did it deliberately and cruelly." Pansy refused to lift her eyes from her book on foot massage and look at John Anderson seated opposite her on the end seat of the railroad car. "The three of us could have overpowered him. And we could have called up Thaddeus and Sidney to help."

"Thaddeus and Sidney, my dear, were probably down in the tower toting dope out to their truck before we got to the top of the stairs."

"Then the three of us could have overpowered him alone."

"One or two of us would most certainly have been shot."

Pansy resumed her reading. John Anderson looked out the window at Rhode Island scrub pine scenery.

Castle, sitting next to Pansy, broke the sullen silence. "I'm still amazed that the police accepted it as an accidental death. I was sure the frayed rope would look suspicious."

John looked at him. "That's what neighbors are for, to confirm worst suspicions. What did that woman from Fifth Road say who was on the news?" He imitated a south Boston accent: "'Holy Mother of Gawd! I told Henry, I told him that guy's gonna fall off one of these days standing up there all

the time. Who does he think he is? The Statue of Liberty?'
Even if she'd seen us up there with him, she would have
sworn Jones had fallen. As it was, there weren't any witnesses, and Maghee couldn't tell the police about Castle's
investigation without getting involved in drug charges. If
Jones was all alone when he fell, it must have been either an
accident or suicide."

"Maghee's probably disappeared by now."

"If he's wise, he has. When the army investigates, they're
going to find out what Donald Jones—Moosa Makki was
doing and go after everyone who worked for him."

Pansy slammed her book closed. "I still say you didn't
have to kill him. Mamadou was bad enough, but two people
dead is a tragedy."

"Zero tolerance for drug kingpins, our official policy," replied Anderson.

"That means confiscating a yacht when you find someone
on board smoking a joint, not pushing people off roofs without a trial. What if he wasn't Moosa Makki?"

"Ah! So that's what you're worried about. You think Moosa
Makki is still lurking somewhere to steal your violin. Castle,
you're a man of sober judgment. Do you think our Donald
Jones was Moosa Makki?"

"Oh, absolutely," said Castle to Pansy. "Ali, or Eldee, told
me I was going to meet Makki, and I called him that to his
face."

"Oh, I know that," said Pansy sharply. "John is deliberately misunderstanding me. I'm not *worried* that Jones
wasn't Moosa Makki. I'm sure he was. I just think it should
have been established legally. Jones could have unraveled
the whole drug operation if he had been arrested."

"My dear, anything he could have unraveled will unravel
anyway. And everything else will stay the same. DJones
Company is gone. But the Pahlavaniya network is still there.
The profits are still there. Shaykh Zack or Moosa Makki or
someone like them will always be there. It's what makes the
DEA so much like an order of crusading knights. The Sacred
Knights of the Drug Enforcement Administration. Drugs are

like pure evil. They're always there and always bad. The DEA struggles against evil but can never win because evil is part of human nature. So the struggle itself rather than victory becomes the objective, and the holiness of the objective purifies the knights of sin."

"Purifies the sacred knights of the DEA of sin," scoffed Pansy. "You don't believe for a minute that you were legally or morally justified in pushing Jones off that roof. You just say things like that because you're so full of bullshit you think it's hamburger."

"Well, pretty Pansy, you didn't seem to be too upset about Sidney smacking Eldee with a hammer. That's a third death to add to your tragedy."

"That one was an accident, though. Sidney didn't intend to kill Eldee. He just hit him too hard."

"An accident? Oh, really. When we got to the office, they said he was alive but might have an itsy-bitsy concussion. Remember? What was it Thaddeus said? 'Sidney knows how to hit people.' I guess Sidney wasn't as much an expert as Thaddeus thought. Either that, or while we were going upstairs he bashed him again and finished him off."

Pansy looked at John angrily. "Well, whatever happened to Eldee, I didn't have anything to do with it. But you personally pushed Donald Jones off the roof. There's a *big* difference. Moreover, Eldee had killed Estelle Marie, and Estelle Marie was Thaddeus and Sidney's cousin. He probably killed Arnold Muhammad, too. Donald Jones, on the other hand, hadn't killed anybody. The only person who wanted him dead was Shaykh Zack, who brutally shot poor Castle."

"I suppose, then, that you think killing Mamadou is a worse crime than wholesaling drugs to our nation's impressionable youth. That is not a DEA position. Besides, you're not absolutely sure that Eldee killed either Mamadou or Arnold Muhammad. You just want to believe he did so you won't feel guilty about telling Thaddeus and Sidney to take care of Eldee for you, and then letting them get away."

"We all agreed to let Thaddeus and Sidney get away," said Pansy.

"For God's sake, come off it, you two," interjected Castle nervously. "This is all you've been doing for three days. It's over. We can't change anything. Nobody was going to believe Jones fell by accident if Eldee's body was in the office. Eldee was Thaddeus and Sidney's responsibility. Making them get rid of the body in exchange for letting them keep the drugs in the tower was a very reasonable solution. Otherwise there would have been a murder investigation, and we would all have been in the soup."

"So now, for our convenience and exculpation," replied John, "Eldee Germaine is lying face up on some frozen cranberry bog where Sidney and Thaddeus have thrown him, but I'm expected to feel remorse for giving Donald Jones, a major drug dealer, a little shove."

"I don't care what you say. You didn't have to kill him," murmured Pansy, who had resumed her reading again.

John gave her a superior look. "One, I killed him because he was threatening you and Castle with a gun. Two, I killed him because he was Moosa Makki, and he was going to continue endangering you, Pansy Garden, until he got the violin back."

"Not if he was in jail," mouthed Pansy without looking up from her book.

"And three, I killed him because he was a drug kingpin, and I am an intrepid and highly skilled hunter of drug kingpins. Finish." John turned his head sharply and stared out the window with a look of injured dignity on his face.

Pansy mouthed the word "murderer."

Castle slumped down, put his feet up on the empty seat beside John, and shut his eyes. Pansy was right, he thought, but giving Jones an extra shove was just part of Anderson's style, like inventing Green Mountain Blue and dressing up in exotic costumes.

"Where are we?" said Castle, waking up in a dimmed car.

"New Haven. They turn the lights out while they switch from electric to diesel. Or the other way 'round."

"Where's John?"

"In the john."

"I'm back," said John as he reappeared from behind Castle's shoulder and swung into his seat. The lights suddenly came back on.

"Another hour and a half? Two hours?" queried Castle.

"Something like that," said John. He turned toward Pansy. "What's the plan for meeting Frankie?"

"He lives in Queens. So I agreed to meet on his territory. I called him twice. It's all arranged. He just doesn't want me to say exactly where it is. He's very nervous, especially since I told him that Estelle Marie and Eldee were both dead. So we'll let him do it his way. But don't worry. He has the violin. We'll get it."

"And then we give it back to the police," added Castle. "That part I insist on. I don't care if the police decide to give it to you or to the DEA or to whoever. I just want to clear that up."

"It belongs to Shaykh Zack," said John. "Don't you think I should take it back to Oman with me?"

Pansy shrugged. "Personally, I don't think a man who shoots visitors in the thighs and leaves them to die deserves much consideration. But if the marvelous DEA wants Shaykh Zack to have it back, it makes no difference to me. We'll give it to the police, and you can get it from them. Then it will be official, and Castle and I will be out of it."

"If you do give it to Shaykh Zack, find out what the message says and send it to me," added Castle hopefully. "That will be the true end of our quest, won't it, Pansy?"

Pansy gave Castle a patronizing look. "John was being facetious. And to tell you the truth, Snaggletooth, three dead bodies have cooled my enthusiasm for questing. I just want to get rid of the damn thing and forget about it."

"And then what will you two lovebirds do? Get married? Breed? A castle soaring high in the midst of the garden? A delicate pansy brightening up the gloom of winter? Little snaggletoothed boys and girls with mohawks running around?"

"Incredibly beautiful snaggletoothed boys and girls with mohawks and completely unlined, youthful-looking faces, if you please," replied Pansy. She turned toward Castle. "John's jealous. Did you know that, Castle? Have you ever had anyone jealous of you over a woman before? Except your orthodontist, maybe, if he thought he had something going with his hygienist."

"Judith had a very professional relationship with her employer," said Castle.

"Jealousy is not part of my makeup," sniffed John.

"Neither are snips and snails and puppy dog tails," said Castle.

"That's enough from you, Snags."

"Stop!" interrupted Pansy holding up her hands. "It's my fault! I never should have brought the subject up. Let's just drop it and sit quietly until we get to New York." Pansy took her Walkman out of her purse and placed its tiny earphones over her head. Wee musical noises drifted forth. The train started to move.

"I hate music," said Castle under his breath as he settled back into his snoozing position.

John Anderson stared out the window at the passing parade of bizarre postmodern architecture. He thought about the arid mountains, medieval fortresses, and gloriously costumed people of Oman.

22

Pansy telephoned Frankie from a pay phone in Pennsylvania Station to say they were on their way. Castle couldn't understand how she had managed for a month out of one small suitcase when he was loaded down with two large ones. He envied John's wheeled suitcase as they walked through endless underground corridors past video arcades, donut shops, pizzerias, and hot dog emporia toward the subway.

"We'll take the Broadway Local to Times Square and then change to the Flushing line," said Pansy, leading the way. "I've got tokens."

During the short ride from Penn Station to Times Square, Castle deciphered a Spanish language advertisement for cockroach exterminator and started on another that purported to speak man to man about the use of condoms. Pansy listened to music and stared anxiously into space. John looked around with interest at the sparse scattering of Sunday evening riders.

At Times Square Castle trailed Pansy and John down a flight of stairs and around a corner. He lost sight of them as he passed a newstand and was momentarily confused. Signs pointed toward the A and E trains but not to the Flushing Line. Then he saw John and Pansy disappearing down another flight of stairs with the sign 7 FLUSHING LINE above it. His arms were tiring of the heavy suitcases.

166

Pansy and John were waiting at the bottom of the stairs.

"Keep up, Castle," said Pansy impatiently. "We almost lost you." She turned and set off down the platform with John. Castle put his bags down to rest his arms.

Suddenly a strangely beautiful sound, magnified by the echoing tunnel, came floating from the distant end of the platform. It was the sound of a violin, but at the same time of more than a violin, a fuller, more poignant sound that with purity and simplicity conveyed a sense of mortal anguish and immortal vision. John Anderson stopped abruptly and let go of his suitcase, his hands half rising at his sides as if he were about to receive an embrace.

"Castle, John recognizes the violin!" screamed Pansy. "He's Moosa Makki!"

John had started running toward the unseen source of the music at the end of the platform. Pansy hesitated and then dropped her own suitcase and ran after him, her earphones still clamped on her head. Castle started forward and then remembered his suitcases.

The platform was bordered by a seemingly endless succession of massive dark green I-beam pillars beside the sunken tracks on either side. Staircases and escalators regularly spaced down the middle blocked any view of what was at the end. John had run almost a hundred yards when he passed the last staircase. The end of the platform was an open area nine yards wide and twenty yards long terminating in a white tiled wall. A short, thin Hispanic youth wearing a blue beret was standing in front of the wall playing the violin. Around him, facing down the platform with folded arms, were a half dozen larger, huskier Hispanic youths wearing identical berets. Beyond the perimeter of their phalanx five subway passengers were standing motionless in rapt fascination.

John stopped at the large square trash bins under the last staircase and pulled a gun from under his coat.

"Give me the violin!" he shouted. "Give me the violin, and no one will get hurt!" Frankie kept on playing, his companions unfolded their arms and scowled. John walked forward, shifting the aim of his gun from one blue-bereted youth to another. "It's my violin, and you don't know how to play it. Give it to me. I don't want to hurt anyone." The five passengers seemed oblivious to the commotion as they continued to face Frankie, absorbed in the beauty of the music.

"It's only a toy gun, Frankie!" yelled Pansy, coming into sight from behind the staircase. "Grab him, you guys! He murdered somebody!"

The cohort of Hispanic youths spread out till they covered the width of the platform. They moved slowly forward, two of them with knives in their hands. John Anderson stopped. He turned and aimed the gun at a metal trash bin behind him. The sound of the gunshot was explosive in the confined space. Pansy ducked behind the staircase as the Hispanic youths halted in their tracks.

"It's not a toy," said John, resuming his walk forward. He looked from youth to youth. "I don't want to hurt anybody. I just want my violin." Frankie's bodyguard warily backed away at his approach. He reached out to Frankie. "Give it to me, kid. Come on. Give it to me, and I'll show you how it should be played."

"I'm playing beautiful," replied Frankie.

John leveled the gun at Frankie's head. "Give it to me," he said softly, "or I will shoot a hole in your head."

Frankie stopped bowing the violin and lowered it. John put his gun in his belt and took the violin and bow.

"Now I'll show you how it should be played," he said as he turned on the ring of blue berets cautiously advancing again upon him.

John put the violin under his chin and drew the bow across its strings. The sound that welled forth opened the gates of paradise and revealed God in His glory. The ethereal, mesmerizing loveliness of Frankie's music was dwarfed by the music of heavenly bliss and life everlasting.

Frankie's mouth opened in amazement as he stood frozen in place. His bodyguards stopped moving forward. Their eyes lost focus, or found new focus, in the purity of God's eternal light. Playing like he had never done anything else in his life, John walked calmly past them and past the equally rapt passengers. With the deep creases of his face drawn up in a smile, he, too, seemed charmed by the mystic sound, but he was also in control. The power was his.

As he passed the first staircase, Pansy flew out at him like a wild animal and grabbed him around the waist. The momentum of her rush rocked him on his feet. He took three staggering steps toward the pit of the subway track and was teetering on its edge when he reached out with his bow hand and caught the flange of a giant I-beam. Pansy leaned all her weight into him, driving her feet into the concrete as she struggled to push him over the edge. Freed from the music, the blue berets were racing up the platform. John's grip on the I-beam tightened. He steeled his powerful muscles and pulled himself upright, at the same time reaching down with the hand holding the violin and plucking Pansy's earphones from her auburn mane. With a powerful countershove he pushed her away from him.

Pansy crouched before him, panting. "I'll shoot you, John," she warned with a shaking voice. His gun was in her hand pointed at his midsection.

John glanced at the Hispanic bodyguards who were now standing on either side of her glowering at him. In a single lightning move he swept the violin to his chin and powered the bow across the strings. A gunshot exploded, and a bullet smashed into the white tiles on the far side of the subway track behind him. But there was no second shot. Pansy and the bodyguards stood riveted in place, their eyes fixed on a vision not of this world. The gun drooped in her slack hand. Frankie, in the background, began to do a slow turning dance.

John played for a few moments and then walked calmly away from his tormentors. As he passed each staircase he saw people who had begun to descend frozen in mid-step, where they had suddenly halted at the sound of the music. Three were policemen with drawn guns. John smiled and played an air he had composed that caused people to see glories that Shaykh Zack could never have imagined: the four rivers of paradise rippling forth from a crystal pool amidst Eden's verdant garden, and in the center of the pool, the foaming fountain of eternal life itself. Tears came to his eyes as he contemplated the beauty of it.

He passed one staircase and then another. His frozen pursuers looked like oddly postured dolls at the far end of the platform. As he turned to go up the final staircase a heavy suitcase swung at his head from behind and caught him with its hard corner. John smashed against the side of the stairs and recoiled off them to see Castle Winter lunge from behind a trash bin. Castle swung the suitcase again, and it breezed within an inch of his face. The momentum of the powerful swing pulled Castle's body sideways until he was facing the tracks. As Castle turned again toward John and collected himself for another attack, John stepped backward and calmly put the violin to his chin. The music of the spheres soared forth and mingled in uncanny harmony with the roar of an approaching train. Like an Olympic hammer thrower Castle whirled all the way around twice with extended arms and let the heavy suitcase fly. The missile's full force landed crushingly on John's chest. He reeled sideways toward the lip of the track flailing his arms. An instant too late he dropped the violin. The tips of his fingers hooked on the edge of a green I-beam and then slipped off. The front of the train roaring out of the tunnel caught his body in mid-air as it fell from the platform and bore him broken like a stringless puppet to the far end of the station.

Castle picked up the violin undamaged from the suitcase it had fallen on.

23

Pansy's apartment was one big room in the East Village. The woodwork around the windows and doors was painted pink, and large pink hearts were painted here and there on the white walls. The polished hardwood floor was bare. Frankie walked around and looked at things: a Barbie doll collection on a dresser, a herd of My Little Ponies on top of the refrigerator, a scuffed up dollhouse with old-looking wooden furniture. Pansy and Castle were sitting on her bed, which was covered by a pink bedspread edged with little white puffballs.

"Why didn't you tell me you were tone deaf?" asked Pansy.

"After telling you about my teeth, I was afraid to," replied Castle sheepishly. "It's one of those things I have a hangup about."

"You can't hear music at all?"

"It's all just noise. It's a terrible defect. You can't imagine what it's like to grow up in a generation devoted to rock music and not be able to hear it."

"God, if I'd only known. Frankie warned me on the phone that hearing him play made people freak out until they got used to it. That's why I kept my earphones on when we got into the station."

Castle looked at her reproachfully. "You should have told

me what was going on. You and Frankie should never have tried to trap John alone."

"What would you have done if I had told you?"

Castle didn't answer.

"I'll tell you what you would have done. First, you wouldn't have believed that John was Moosa Makki. And then, if you had believed me, you would have gotten so antsy that John would have caught on that something was up. That train trip from Boston was an excruciating experience. I couldn't keep myself from telling John what I thought of him. And then, even if you hadn't tipped him off somehow, you still would have insisted on guarding your goddam suitcases."

"Well, what did you expect me to do? You can't just leave suitcases lying around unattended in a New York subway station. They get stolen."

"But what about after you heard the gunshot?"

"You don't run *toward* a gunshot in the subway, Pansy. You run away from it. How did I know it had to do with you and John? You told me he only had a fake gun."

Pansy mused. Frankie had settled down in a yellow bean-bag chair with a stack of comic books entitled V *for Vendetta*.

"He did fool me about the gun," said Pansy at length. "His problem was that he had to kill Donald Jones before Jones did anything to show that he recognized John. I mean, supposing John had come out on the roof with a gun in his hand and Jones had said, 'Hey, Moosa, how ya doing? I'm holding these guys here just like you wanted.'"

"Would have given it away," agreed Castle. "But I still can't believe he would kill his own man just to get the violin back."

"That's because you couldn't hear the way he played it. It gave him unbelievable power. I couldn't move. No one could move except Frankie. Even people who were looking right at you when you threw the suitcase at him didn't see it. They were in heaven. We were all in heaven."

"Lucky thing for me. Second time in a week someone was pushed to his death with no witnesses."

"I can play it even better than him, Pansy. Believe me. Put you in heaven plus. I know how to do it now." Frankie offered his comments from the beanbag chair without taking his eyes from his comic book.

"Lotsa luck."

"I mean it. I'll practice. I'm making a couple hundred bucks a day just playing the stuff I already know down in the subway. Then in the evening I play for the guys. Practice like that, use some of the man's tunes, I'll be at Carnegie Hall in no time."

"I guess it's better for Frankie to keep the violin than to give it back to Shaykh Zack," said Castle. "Unless the Pahlavanis come looking for him."

"I can take care of myself," said Frankie confidently. "The guys will protect me. We're gonna start our own Sufi order, too, whatever that is." He put his comic book down. "Actually, I think someone should tell me more about this Sufi stuff. I coulda got killed, and I still don't know what that was all about."

"Want me to tell you?" said Pansy. "I'll tell you. You know that John was a real hotshot with the violin. I don't mean to take anything away from you, but he was into it for a lot longer time. While he was working as a narc in Oman, he became a member of this religious brotherhood called the Pahlavaniya. In the brotherhood he used the name Moosa Makki, and he was so good at disguising himself that they probably didn't even know who he really was. Anyway, meditating and chanting and religious stuff like that came real easy to him, and he thought he should be the next leader. To become the leader he had to be picked by the current leader, Shaykh Zack, and given a new violin with the charm written in it. But Shaykh Zack picked someone else. So John got pissed off and stole the violin.

"Since John worked for the DEA and knew all about drug dealing, he knew that Shaykh Zack and some of the other

Pahlavanis were into that. So after he stole the violin, John took some leave from his job and came back to the United States. A couple of American Pahlavanis he had met in Oman came with him. They were Moe Maghee and Ali Abdussalam, the big guy we saw at the police station. His original name was Eldee Germaine.

"John couldn't try to take over everything from Shaykh Zack without everyone knowing he was a thief, so he decided instead to set up a drug smuggling operation using just a few Pahlavanis. Moe Maghee and Eldee Germaine helped him recruit members, and most of them were happy to join once they heard John play the violin. They found Donald Jones, who had become a member of the order in San Francisco, and made him the front man. Since John was still with the DEA, he knew all about the army's drug program, and he figured out a way to use it to cover his smuggling.

"Things went okay for almost two years. Then Arnold Muhammad Mustafa, who was a Muslim friend of Eldee Germaine's, stole the violin. Shaykh Zack had spread the word there was a big reward, and Arnold went for it. Arnold was living with Mamadou in her apartment, and Mamadou helped him steal the violin.

"Before Arnold and Mamadou could hand over the violin and get the reward, her cousins Sidney and Thaddeus got busted using her apartment, and the police took the violin. Then the police held it for weeks, waiting for the grand jury. Arnold got worried that he would never get it back so he called in to say a violin with Arabic writing in it had been stolen. He probably used the name M. Mustafa so it would be harder to connect him with Mamadou, who had the lease on the apartment where the violin was."

"This gonna go on all day, Pansy?" interjected Frankie. "I think I heard enough."

"No, go on, Pansy," said Castle. "It's fascinating to hear it all put together."

Frankie resumed reading V for Vendetta.

"That's okay. You know the rest, Castle. Eldee, or somebody, killed Arnold Muhammad, and then Eldee and

Mamadou went down to the police station posing as M. Mustafa to try to get it when the police released it."

"Was Mamadou really her name?" said Frankie, looking up.

"No. Estelle Marie Whitehead. Go back to your comic."

"Why'd she call herself Mamadou?"

"How should I know? Maybe she liked it. It suited her. But the main thing was that she had to be M. Mustafa at the police station to claim the violin because that's the name Arnold Muhammad had used in reporting it stolen."

"Why wasn't John doing all this?" asked Castle.

"Because he was in Oman, obviously. He was there when you arrived. My guess is, when the violin was stolen, it was obvious that whoever stole it would be sending it or selling it back to Shaykh Zack. John told Eldee to work on finding out who stole the violin at this end, and he headed back to Oman hoping to intercept the violin there before Shaykh Zack could get it back."

"It must have been risky posing as a guard."

"Well, you know John. He loved to dress up. I imagine he counted on everyone assuming that Moosa Makki would stay as far away from Oman as possible. They must not have associated him before with the American advisor in the date factory. He probably decided he could pull off one more scam."

"Okay. So then I got shot, and he brought me back to New York and abandoned me."

"Right. He knew you didn't know where the violin was. But from what you had told him, he figured that I did. So he came looking for me. And where did he find me? A block away from his own company, which I had ingeniously sleuthed out while you were gone. It confirmed his suspicions."

"But that doesn't explain how he came to be living with you."

"That, Castle, is an exciting but seamy story that I never intend to tell you. The reason he wanted to be with me, though, is obvious. I knew where the violin was. He wanted the violin. He had to find a way to persuade me to tell him.

175

But I stoically withstood even the most sordidly erotic means of persuasion because I was always true to you, Castle. I had sworn that only you would ever get my violin."

"I'd appreciate it if you'd swear a similar oath about your body."

"I'll proceed. Since he couldn't coax me to tell or scare me into telling by warning me about Moosa Makki, he improvised. He brought you into the picture to get at me. If you were in danger, maybe I would tell. Or maybe I'd tell you, and he could get it out of you. I'm not sure he ever really thought it out carefully. But eventually he decided that the only way to break me down was to pretend to kill Moosa Makki. Poor Donald Jones was his victim. He never anticipated his buddy Eldee Germaine being killed, of course, because Thaddeus and Sidney were wild cards who just happened along."

"So at the end John stage-managed everything."

"Everything. It was complicated because he had to work it so we got up to the roof while Jones was holding you there, and then make it look like Jones's death was accidental so there wouldn't be a police investigation. That's why he couldn't use his gun."

"Well, I'll be damned. How did you figure all this out?"

"Text adventures. I'm real good at them, particularly mapping. When you get into the adventure, you go north, and then east, and then north, and then north again, and then west, and so on. At every stop there's a description of a room, and you can quickly lose track of where you are and go around in circles missing some obvious option. So you map it, and that solves most of your problems. I should show you the charts I made of this one, the 'Violin Quest.' You'd be amazed."

"And your maps told you that John was really Moosa Makki?"

"Of course."

"What do you mean, 'of course'? Give me an example of something that made you think John was really Moosa."

"One thing? There were a lot of things. For example,

every time he told his story about Shaykh Zack, and you being shot, and him rescuing you, it didn't quite make sense. But it always mapped out the same way: Moosa Makki was going to be eliminated, and John was going to end up with the violin. And then I was particularly suspicious because he didn't know what Makki looked like. That was probably a mistake. I think he should have made up something that would point to Donald Jones. But originally I don't believe he meant to kill Jones, so he might have thought it was better to keep it vague. I made it easier to improvise."

"Don't forget to tell about the Harvard Class Report," said Frankie.

"What was that?" asked Castle.

"John was so full of bullshit I called Frankie and asked him to check out his story about being a Harvard graduate, and Peace Corps, and all that. It all turned out to be true."

Frankie pulled a folded piece of paper out of his pocket. "Here's this from the Class Report fifteen years after he got out of school. I ripped it outta the book. It says:

"*John Draggon Anderson: Factory manager; Oman National Date Company, Nizwa, Oman. You may breathe easier, dear classmates, for knowing that the narc in your midst is aspiring to loftier goals. I have at long last found inner peace as a follower of Shaykh Zakariya ibn Muhammad Pahlavani, the Supreme Guide of the Pahlavaniya Sufi brotherhood. I lead a quiet life here among the date groves nailing smugglers and communing occasionally with my Sufi brethren. Since it is almost impossible for anyone to get a visa to Oman, I shall forbear from inviting my classmates to come and visit. In fact, to quote a great Harvard man who said it better than I can, 'I have changed, outwardly or inwardly, to the point that my college friends would not easily recognize my face and the mask behind it.' Peace.*"

Castle looked puzzled. "How did that tip you off that he was Moosa Makki?"

Pansy smiled triumphantly. "John made a mistake. To make it plausible that he didn't know what Moosa Makki looked like, he gave us a long bullshit story and then told me privately that he wasn't a Pahlavani. But I had a special way of determining that he was lying so from that moment on I became suspicious of him."

"How could you tell he was lying?"

"I never intend to divulge that secret to you, Castle. But to continue, when Frankie found out John had boasted to his classmates about being a Pahlavani, I decided to test him in the subway. If he recognized the music, it would mean that he really was a Pahlavani and that he had heard Shaykh Zack play the violin in Oman. Therefore he would have to have known, or been able to find out, what Moosa Makki looked like. The only explanation for his lying would then be that he was Moosa Makki himself."

Castle shook his head slowly.

"I'll show you the maps. It'll make it easier."

"No. I think I get it. I was just thinking that if he had been able to win the favor of Shaykh Zack, he might have become the next leader of the Pahlavaniya and a great saint. He would probably never have become a drug smuggler or a murderer."

"He might have anyway," said Pansy. "Maybe the reason Shaykh Zack didn't pick him was because he thought he wouldn't make a good saint."

Castle was silent. "Well, in the long run, who cares?" he said at last. "The quest remains, and that's the important thing."

Pansy looked at Castle quizzically. "The quest?"

Castle sat up straight and looked down his nose at her imperiously. "It did not escape your notice that John's middle name was Draggon, I assume? Therefore, have I not killed my dragon and rescued my princess?"

"You killed a fellow human being by knocking him in front of a subway train. I'm not sure that is exactly slaying a dragon, Castle."

"And now that that obstacle is overcome," continued Castle grandly, "it is time to go for the final quest."

"The violin message?" said Pansy in a small, puzzled voice.

"We shall go together to the southern Philippines, to the island of Palawan, and there seek out old and wise men who know the secrets of the ancient writing. They shall be delighted that we have found our way to them and at last introduce us into the mysteries of the violin's message, which we shall bear as secret knowledge to our graves."

"But first we'll live long lives in tropical paradise and raise little buck-toothed, tone-deaf children?" said Pansy hopefully.

"And teach our disciples the ways of knowledge," intoned Castle.

"And maybe open a little computer software store?"

"We'll need it to pay for the orthodontist, won't we?"

Frankie studiously perused his murderous and gruesome comic book and shut his ears to the sounds of sighs and kissing.

THE END

Afterword

Although the people, places, and events in this story are purely fictitious, the violin around which it revolves is not. Sometime in the spring of 1968, someone living in the Boston area took a violin—a rather bad-looking, poorly varnished violin—to a violin maker for restoration. The violin maker removed the top of the violin and discovered, written in pencil on the inside of the backboard, the same inscription reproduced in the story.

The owner of the violin, whose name I never learned, took the instrument to the Hebrew Division of Widener Library at Harvard University in hopes of having someone decipher the writing. The chief Hebrew cataloguer, recognizing the script to be Arabic, took the violin across the hall to his colleague Labib Zuwiyya-Yamak, the head of the library's Middle East Division. Labib looked at it with amusement. Even though the writing was clear, not a single word was decipherable—except, of course, for the name Muhammad in line 5. The same name possibly recurs in line 6, but there as elsewhere portions of words are obscured by glue.

Labib thought perhaps a child had written the meaningless words, but he was amused and copied them down. That evening Harvard's Middle East Center, where I then had my office, had scheduled a lecture by a distinguished guest—I have no recollection who it was—and a number of faculty and students were invited to a dinner to honor him at the Harvard Faculty Club. I sat beside Labib, and during the dinner he pulled out the piece of paper upon which he had written the violin message.

The inscription meant nothing to me either, but then I am not a great philologist. What was astonishing was that none of the three or four senior professors the paper circulated among on our wing of the table could read a single word of it. I later tried to reconstruct how many languages that gifted group of scholars knew collectively, and I am sure it could not have been fewer than fifty, including almost every language commonly written in Arabic script.

Intrigued by the materialization of such a mystery, which curiously no one else seemed to take any cognizance of, I examined the violin the next day in Labib's office. Aside from the one technical flaw in its manufacture mentioned in the story, the extra groove filed in the nut, I could see nothing distinctive about it. But I copied the message, reproducing its very distinctive version of the Arabic script as carefully as I could, and resolved to find out, somehow, somewhere, what it said.

I never saw the violin again. I never asked who owned it. Labib Zuwiyya-Yamak was tragically taken by an early death. I do not know if any of the professors who first saw the message has any recollection of the event. It seemed to make no impression on them at the time, and twenty-some years have now elapsed.

But over those two decades of following hunches and presenting the problem to myriad scholars, I have never discovered what language the message is in or what it says. Having ruled out so many languages—all of those mentioned in chapter 5—I am left with the southern Philippines, the possibility used as a basis for the story. Did some Bostonian serve in the army that fought against native forces there after the United States wrested control of the islands from Spain in 1898? Did he bring home a locally produced violin, a copy of a European violin perhaps, as a war souvenir? Did his family forget, three generations later, where "that old violin" came from?

The shapes of the script resemble specimens of Arabic produced in the southern Philippines. The limited number of consonants seems appropriate for the languages of the Malayo-Polynesian family that predominate in the area. The

symbol, which probably represents the sound *ng*, apparently borrows its top portion from a similar mark in Sanskrit and Hindi. Sanskrit is the classical Indian language that heavily influenced the pre-Islamic culture of Indonesia, whence Islam and the Arabic script reached the Philippines some five centuries ago. I have also learned that European-style violins were made locally in Southeast Asia, including the Philippines, earlier in this century.

But these slight indications are no substitute for a translation of the inscription and an explanation for its being hidden inside a violin.

So what was I to do? Write a small article for the *Journal of the American Oriental Society*? I might have gotten a result; I might not. It would certainly have been a boring way to proceed.

Instead I decided to write *The Sufi Fiddle*. Since professors are not able to offer magnificent rewards, I cannot offer treasure to the person or persons who provide me with an accurate and verifiable translation of the inscription and thus end my quest. But they will earn my deepest thanks and an expression of appreciation in any subsequent edition of this book.